D1472899

The Book of Joshua

THE
BOOK
of
JOSHUA

Jennifer Anne Moses

The University of Wisconsin Press

The University of Wisconsin Press
1930 Monroe Street, 3rd Floor
Madison, Wisconsin 53711-2059
uwpress.wisc.edu

3 Henrietta Street, Covent Garden
London WCE 8LU, United Kingdom
eurospanbookstore.com

Printed in the United States of America

This book may be available in a digital edition.

Library of Congress Cataloging-in-Publication Data

Names: Moses, Jennifer Anne, author.
Title: The book of Joshua / Jennifer Anne Moses.
Description: Madison, Wisconsin: The University of Wisconsin Press, [2018]
Identifiers: LCCN 2018011390 | ISBN 9780299319502 (cloth: alk. paper)
Subjects: | LCGFT: Novels. | Fiction.
Classification: LCC PS3563.O88437 B66 2018 | DDC 813/.54—dc23
LC record available at https://lccn.loc.gov/2018011390

This is a work of fiction. Names, characters, businesses, places, events, locales, and incidents are either the products of the author's imagination or used in a fictitious manner. Any resemblance to actual persons, living or dead, or actual events is purely coincidental. The author would moreover like to acknowledge that mental illness and its treatments are treated fictitiously in this novel. For example, the drug combinations that the protagonist talks about sprang from the author's imagination as filtered through internet searches. No part of the novel is intended to reflect or be a substitute for the medical advice of a licensed physician.

For

Jerry Weiss

friend, mentor, mensch

The Book of Joshua

Prologue

What challenge, experience, situation, or encounter have you had to overcome, and how has that event or set of events shaped you into becoming the kind of person you want to be in college? —The Collective University App, option 4

1

Dear Admissions Committee:

I recently read an article in the newspaper that said that more and more high school seniors are writing essays about things like their penises. Or the trauma of walking in on their parents in mid-private-parental activity. Or the year they spent eating their own toe fungus. The point of the article is that there are kids so desperate to go to their first-choice college that they'll write about just about anything in order to stand out against the crowd of your usual overachieving "the year I volunteered in an AIDS hospital in Somalia"-type essays. Whereas the best I can do in the brag-a-sphere is the following: I eventually passed all my classes. *All* of them. Including the one I hated.

But if you're serious, and actually intend to read my application essay and not just throw it out based on my somewhat less-than-exemplary grades, I will tell you that though I have never founded my own organic lettuce farm or helped build a rural hospital in a war-torn country on the other side of the globe, I can beat out just about anyone for sheer awful unparalleled and original weirdness.

In short, for about a year, the future of humanity rested on my shoulders, and that's because I had been chosen to save the world. I knew, because I was given instructions by various Voices, which sounded like human voices, only a thousand times more powerful, with a depth of beauty impossible to replicate. And part of what I now understand to be a terrible hallucination was pretty good. The other part, not so much.

In any event, being endowed with supernatural powers changed me, which perhaps is obvious, given that, duh, it's not every day of the week that suddenly, *kerpoof*, you're teleported from this pretty normal middle-class suburban existence in northern New Jersey to being selected to save the world. Forget about college—who needed a college degree when I was headed straight for omnipotent nirvana? Even so, after my stint as the hope of humankind was over, I didn't really think a whole heck of a lot about college at all. Instead, my plans for the future involved—not so much. Drooling. Eating donuts. Porn. The usual post-nuthouse kind of thing.

And the worst of it? Even though I had been told about my super-human days, about what I'd done or said, I myself couldn't remember any of it. All I knew was that I had somehow disposed of my left eye, and that my girlfriend, the girl I loved, Sophie—the last person I remember seeing before I woke up in the hospital with bandages on my face—was untraceable, as in vanished, as in abducted by aliens, as in *gone*. So yeah, I had only one eye, my girlfriend had vanished, and on top of everything else, I still had to live.

2

One of the thousands of conditions of my coming home after weeks in the psych ward and then a few additional weeks in a post-psych-ward transitional housing program was that I attend meetings with other youthful nut cases. The meetings, officially called Teens in Transition Support Systems (or TITSS, a ridiculously hilarious acronym that apparently never occurred to the various MDs and PhDs who came up with it), were held in a window-free conference room in a hospital conveniently located a mere three miles from my house.

It was late June when I came home, meaning that half of everyone I had ever known was away, and the other half was hunkering down inside their air-conditioned rec rooms. Hot and humid and dazed with heavy gray: not a creature was stirring. It was like living in a post-apocalyptic freeze-frame, except with carry-out Chinese and pizza, with which I stuffed my face, eating being the only thing that made me feel like I wasn't completely dead. That and cigarettes, which I totally hoped would give me lung cancer ASAP.

TITSS was Dr. Rose's idea. Dr. Rose was my personal, go-and-talk-to psychiatrist, as opposed to Dr. Chang in the hospital where I first came-to *sans* eyeball, and then, in the regular nuthouse treatment program in which I was confined for another eternity, doctors Husak, Larimar, O'Leary, Grossman, and, I mess with you not, Aswad. I liked Dr. Rose, but because I had lost my driver's license sometime around the time I lost my eye, Mom had to take me there, which was just depressing as hell, something that Dr. Rose seemed unperturbed by when I went on about it. "At your age, she's supposed to drive you crazy," he would say before asking me a dozen questions about my meds and my weight and my feelings about food and sex and my brother and my childhood and my dreams and my ability to make kaka. "She's your *mother.*"

In addition to eating, there was one other activity that I regularly did: I would climb up to the attic to gaze at a picture I had of Sophie and me that was taken of us when we first met, at summer camp. I didn't go up there alone, either. I went with Athens. Athens was a stuffed brown dog, about nine inches tall. Someone gave him to me when I was an infant. For years, he had been living in the linen closet. But since I'd returned home, he'd become my best, and only, friend. Unlike my parents, Athens didn't condemn me for my obsession with Sophie. In fact, he shared it. Like everything else related to her, the photo—it was of the two of us, grinning—was contraband. It was something of a miracle that I had succeeded in hiding it from my parents' endless scrutiny by putting it under a loose floorboard under the pile of suitcases in the attic. Together, Athens and I studied the photo, cried, and contemplated the beauties of suicide without fear of interruption or discovery. I had additional contraband up there too, namely, several packs of cigarettes and a lighter. I had hidden them in the outer pocket of a beat-up old suitcase that no one ever used.

"So yeah," I told Dr. Rose. "Athens and me, we hang out in the attic. We like it there."

His diagnosis: "It sounds like you're drowning in loneliness."

"We talk about the best way to commit suicide. I mean, theoretically, ontologically, and philosophically speaking . . ."

"Theoretically?" said Dr. Rose.

"So far, so good."

"It's not funny, Josh. If you mean it, if you're seriously feeling like you want to put an end to things—"

And while he scratched his forehead, I interrupted with an overly cheerful "No worries, Doc!"

"And that photo—that photo of Sophie? How much time do you spend just looking at it?"

He was smart. Also bald, portly, and allergic to cats.

"You're not going to tell my mother, right?"

He scratched his nose, crossed and recrossed his legs. "I think it would be wise for you to start socializing again, with real people, and not just a photo. In a safe environment. With people who won't judge you, because they've been there themselves. Who knows? You might even like it."

"I hang out with Buster." Buster is our dog, an ancient, overweight yellow lab. He lies in the sun all day and farts. We have two cats too, but they exist primarily to snub me.

"I mean with people. Live people. The kind who talk back."

Which is how I ended up at TITSS.

At my first meeting, in July, I was surprised when the first person I saw was Susan, who had been a fellow inmate at the same nuthouse—I mean residential treatment facility—I had been in. Noticing me notice her, she made her eyes into slits.

During our weeks together at the nuthouse, Susan and I would occasionally be in the same room, nodding off in front of the same TV, or gazing through the window of the vending machines at the Cheddar Cheese Puffs, the Chex Mix, the Doritos, and my own personal favorite, the Drake's Apple Fruit Pie. But we never actually spoke, or even exchanged glances. The fact is, Susan didn't even seem aware of her surroundings, or any of the people in it. She never actually got anything out of the vending machines. She hardly even ate.

Though she was visibly bony, with buzz-cut black hair, chewed-down fingernails, and a persistent cough, even in the nuthouse, with the glazed-over look we all had, Susan was hot: *hot* hot, with perfect skin, thick hair, a face like a doe's, huge purple-blue eyes, freckles, the whole impossible package, well beyond my league. It wasn't just me who had had a distant, wistful, pathetic kind of crush on her: pretty much all the guys on the ward did. But she was mean, mean as a snake. She would bite you if you came near. I, for one, never so much as thought about trying.

Now I sat as far from her as possible at the cafeteria-style table where the meeting was held, plopping myself at the far end. At first I thought that maybe she hadn't directed her eye-squinting at me at all—that I was being paranoid—but after a kid with blue hair sat down next to her in the one remaining empty chair, Susan gave me the finger.

It was at this point that the sole grown-up in the room came over, said, "Hi, I'm Fleur," and explained that she would be leading the group meeting. "I've heard a lot of good things about you, Josh," she said, squeezing my hands in both of hers. "I'm so glad you decided to join us."

"Yeah."

"We have a phone list, if you want to put your number down. It's in case you want to reach out to someone in the group, or they want to reach out to you."

"Okay, sure."

With long hair in a braid down her back, big white teeth, no makeup, and an open, innocent expression on her perfectly round face, at first Fleur didn't look old enough to be in charge. But on second glance, I picked up a certain authority, a certain robust energy, that marked her as the boss, as the one who was an *adult*.

Clapping for attention, she picked up a notebook and read: "We welcome you to the Wednesday afternoon Teens in Transition Support Systems group meeting, and are glad you're here. Though what you hear here may at first seem confusing, please do keep coming back. Those of us who have suffered from chemical brain function challenges and have lived, for weeks or longer, in an institutional setting, understand as few others can the challenges of reintegrating into regular, and therefore irregularly structured, life. We're here today to help each other, to understand, to learn to trust again, to share openly . . ." blah blah blah, ending with "The topic today is fear. Fear of being sick again. Fear of being normal again. Fear in general, and how to cope with it. Who would like to start?"

No one said a word. Kids did everything else—bit their fingernails, fiddled in their pockets and bags for the cigarettes they were no doubt planning on lighting up the second they were back outside, picked their noses and teeth, bit their lips—the usual array of nervous tics and slightly antisocial behaviors. Finally, after maybe three minutes that felt like half an hour, Susan raised her hand, and for the first time I heard what her speaking voice sounded like: sandpaper.

"It's bad today," she said in her sandpaper voice.

"Bad?" said Fleur.

"Real bad. Real, real bad." She crumpled into herself. "Bad bad. Bad evil. Bad suck bad. Plus," she said, pointing at me, "*that's* here. What's *that thing* doing here?"

I could feel myself turn purple with a mixture of shame and confusion. I wondered what I'd done wrong this time and looked down at my big ugly fat body to see if maybe I'd had an accident that I hadn't been aware of, or perhaps was covered with bird droppings. Maybe my fly was open and my business was all hanging out?

A moment later, Fleur spoke: "Susan, you know that the protocol here is that we keep inside our own head space. No cross-talking, and no finger-pointing either. I'm sorry you're so down, I know we all are. Okay? You're safe here, Susan, but everyone here needs to be safe, not just you." The kid with the blue hair gave Susan a fist bump. "I mean it," Fleur said.

Later, when I'd been around for a while, I learned that the word on Fleur was that she had the patience of an angel, that she had a younger sister or an aunt or a mother who had gone blotto nuts on her and she had decided to devote her own life to helping kids with mental issues, that she even devoted some of her weekend to volunteering at some home in Newark for troubled teens, but my own theory is that after she got her degree in psychiatric social work, the TITSS gig was the only job she could find.

"Sucks if you're a sucker," Susan said.

As the meeting ticked on, there were more stories: about multiple suicide attempts; about waking up in a straitjacket; about people's butthole brothers and cousins and fathers and teachers. I felt like I was stuck in the back of a third-rate theater watching the worst, most boring, and most nonsensical play ever written, but at least no one forced me to say anything. Then we stood up and, holding hands, chanted the following little bit of syrupy stupid, which signaled the end of the meeting: "We are all God's children. We are bigger than our biochemistry! Today is the first day of the rest of our lives! Keep coming back."

As I waited for Mom to come pick me up, I pulled out a brand new, never-before-touched cigarette, lit up, and pulled the caustic smoke into my lungs, thanking the God I don't believe in for nicotine. Then Mom drove up, rolled down the window, and said, "Smoking gives you cancer."

Exactly.

Speaking of Mom: do you have any clue how humiliating it is to have your mother hover over you twenty-four-seven when you're EIGHTEEN YEARS OLD, SIX FOOT THREE, and a DUDE? And to top it all off, she quit her job. Years and years of fighting for the rights of impoverished and victimized and abandoned and abused kids in various courtrooms and social service agencies, and she gave it all up to focus on my neurons, weight, eating habits, and overall mental health/lack thereof.

After that first meeting, Mom started waiting for me in the parking lot, while I sat with the other teen fatsos, cutters, slashers, bulimics, anorexics, delusionals, OCDs, and failed suicidal chain-smokers at TITSS, while Fleur took us through our regular opening ("We're here to help each other, to understand, to learn to trust again, to share openly our sorrows, fears, terrors, and failures as well as our hope, wisdom, strength, and inspiration, and most of all, to reclaim our ability to feel joy and wonder,") and then opened up the floor for truth-telling, which was the term used for spewing anything, whether it made any kind of coherent or logical sense or not.

Everyone said that the TITSS meetings were based on AA meetings, but I went online to see for myself, only to discover the obvious, namely that, instead of alcoholism, each of us teen losers had gone blotto without any help whatsoever from substance abuse. Actually, this too is not an absolute truth, as many of us at TITSS, all victims of our own badly designed neural circuitry, had aided and abetted our tendency toward delusions and other dysfunctional neurotransmission by what's known in the jargon as "self-medicating" and more widely known as "doing drugs." I myself was, once upon a time, quite the partaker of the mighty weed. No longer, however. Now the only drugs I used—

Clozaril
Abilify
Ativan
Luvox

—were taken in varying combinations and doses, as my medical team figured out what worked best for me.

It was these wonder meds, whittled down to just the right so-called drug cocktail, that chased off the Voices. What they didn't do, however, was get rid of the *voices*, small "v"—unending inner chatter that tended to go into all kinds of hysterics at the drop of a hat, saying things like *Give it up Josh you suck and always will suck and why don't you just stick your head in an oven only maybe not because your parents would never forgive themselves except on the other hand they'd probably be relieved and by the way you'll never have sex especially given how fat you are and do you know how gross it is to watch you shovel egg foo mu down your throat?*

"You're not still hearing voices, are you?" said Mom.

"Just yours, Mom."

"Are you okay?"

"Does it look like I'm okay?"

"Oh, honey . . ."

As bad as it was to be a hugely fat teen schizophrenic who couldn't remember nothing about nada, and to have a hover mother so hovering that she may as well have been a Martian spaceship, it was even worse to be a hugely fat teenage schizophrenic who was expected to bond with others of his kind. I went to the TITSS meetings anyway, week after dreary week, *tick-tock-tick-tock*, while Susan sent death rays to me via her huge purple-blue eyes, and occasionally, upon exiting, brushed up past me, saying, "Freak."

3

It was late August—one of those drizzly days when you don't know if you're hot or cold—when Susan raised her hand, stood up like she was going to make a toast, pointed at me, and said, "Why doesn't *that* explain why he won't stop staring at me?"

"What are you talking about?" I said, but I must have said it softly because no one seemed to register my protest.

"And since it thinks it's so much better than us, that it has super-powers and has been chosen to save the world and shit, why is it in the support group and not back in the hospital? Because me? They made me go back to the hospital like three times and all because I saw a slave in the fields behind where I live. Because it's not like I was hearing voices, or having some sick psychotic delusion, either. This slave? I saw him, just standing there, in this field, see, near where I live, and next to him was this mule, and I knew it was a mule and not a donkey because he was too big to be a donkey and also his ears weren't big like a donkey's, and it was obvious that the guy, the slave guy, was pissed off. Like really really pissed off. I'm like: Of course he's pissed off. He's a slave. I would be pissed off too if I were a slave. So I told my psychiatrist about the slave and they stuck me back into the psyche ward and put me on these really awful meds that made me not be able to go to the bathroom, and made my eyesight blurry too, and everything felt dead to me, I was dead inside, and here *that* is and *that thing* just sits there, all creepy, staring at me with its one eye, so yeah, it pisses me off, is what."

"Okay, Susan, thank you, that's enough. You know the rules here. Let's give someone else a turn. Who wants to go next?"

A hand shot up.

"Yes? Elle?"

"I'm feeling the need to burn myself with cigarettes."

"And I'm feeling the need to put my cigarette out in that creep's one creepy eye," said Susan.

"I'm going to ask you to refrain from speaking for the rest of the meeting, and if you can't, you'll need to leave," Fleur said, but it was too late, because Susan had already stomped out, throwing me hate darts as she passed.

If there was one thing I knew I shouldn't do, it was confront her. But a couple of days later, during the post-meeting smoke-a-thon, I went up to Susan and asked her where she got her messed-up intel. Specifically, I said, "Actually, I do not stare at you. I never have. And I don't think I'm better than other people, let alone a person of extraordinary powers who has been chosen to save the world. Alas, I am merely Josh Cushing."

"You're a pretentious douchebag, is what you are."

"The point is, I'm no longer insane. Really. I don't even remember most of it."

"Tell it to army."

"What?"

"I know all about you," she said. "The way you poked your own eye out, making a blood sacrifice to save the world, like you're God, which you aren't, and even if you were, you probably don't want to go back to the hospital. Unless you do."

"I don't," I said.

"Don't what?"

"I don't want to go back to the hospital."

"Good luck with that." She walked away.

"And stop referring to me as *it*," I said, but I was pretty sure she didn't hear me.

When I slid my bulk into the front seat next to her, Mom, as usual, waxed enthusiastic, peppering me with questions that I didn't answer: "Was it a good session? Are you making friends? Learning anything? That Fleur seems great—do you like her, Josh? Is she great? Do you share? Anything you want to talk about now? Darling?"

"Please be quiet. Please? Okay, Mom?"

"Where are you, Josh? Are you even here?"

"I don't want to talk."

"Are you hearing voices again?"

. . . you are so totally screwed and always will be and what's the use anyway. Did you really say you had superpowers? Did you go around saying shit like that? Do you say things like that now and don't even know that you're saying it? But wait, do you want to jerk off? FUCK! WHAT THE FUCK IS WRONG WITH YOU? Mom's staring at you. Susan's right. You're an it. What happened to your eye, what happened to Sophie, and why didn't you kill yourself when you had the chance, except that you can do it now too, if you weren't such a big fat slob coward worthless piece of amoebic slime . . .

"Josh?"

"What?"

"Are you hearing voices?"

"No."

Back at home, I found my brother, Nate, who was holed up in his lair, to tell him about what Susan had said, and ask him if it was true that I'd poked out my own eye.

"I don't know, maybe. You don't remember?"

"No," I said. "If I did, I wouldn't ask."

"Sorry," he said blithely, as if I had asked him if he happened to have any weed I could share.

"Did Mom and Dad say I poked out my own eye?"

He shrugged. "Dunno. Ask them."

"Why would I do that?"

"Because maybe they know?"

"No, I mean, why would I poke out my own eye?"

"Like . . ." He leaned back in his swivel desk chair, all long and lanky and hyperaware of the fact that for once in our lives as brothers he had the upper hand. "Maybe you were nuts?"

"I know I was nuts. But what happened to my eye? Did I poke it out?"

"Guess you *could* have."

My baby brother: nearly as tall as me but not fat, with elongated, spastic arms and legs like the tentacles on an octopus, fourteen months my junior, convinced that wearing black Converse All Stars made him cool, almost as good a cross-country runner as I was before I went and had what my vast team of psychiatrists refers to as my "schizophrenic break," and downright confused. Both of us were now in our senior year of high school, everyone watching him all the time to see if he was going to turn into another me. A part of me felt sorry for him: no wonder he sometimes acted like such a jerk. A part of me thought he was simply a jerk, born and bred, down to the bone.

"Plus you used to go around spouting all this end-of-the-world shit."

"Do I talk like that now?

Another shrug. Then this weird expression, part smirk, part sympathetic smile.

"*Do I?*"

"How should I know?"

"Because you live here and I do too?"

"I don't know, man. No, I don't think so. Whatever. Who cares?"

I just stared at him, astonished by his total lack of giving-a-shit. Then I began to cry.

"Jesus wept," said my brother.

A true comic genius.

Down the hall, in my own room, I put my fist through the wall, not enough to make a dent, just enough to inflict burning pounding pain into the knuckles and joints of my hand, up through my wrist and elbow, and along my shoulder and upper back.

Which is when Athens said, "Oh, Josh. Let's me and you go to the attic."

I liked it up there, in the attic. I liked the way the air smelled like burnt dust. I liked the way the trapped heat muffled my breathing. I liked being able to hide among the boxes and the loose slabs of roofing insulation. I liked being able to look at Sophie's picture.

4

When I went back to school in the fall, where for a second time I was enrolled as a senior, I was still the big huge fat pale sweating slob that I had been when I first got out of the hospital, so you would think that kids, seeing me, would run in the other direction. Instead, not only did they not run; they didn't even stare. They just kind of turned away, toward the lockers, as if they had urgent business to conduct, or ambled away just a little more quickly, or glanced my way for a fraction of a split second before turning their attention elsewhere, as if they had just *happened* to catch a glimpse of me, by mistake, the way you catch a glimpse of dog-doo, or two insects mating. It wasn't surprising, though: most kids at Western High, Nate and me included, had been taught since birth not to stare at exactly the kind of people you want to stare at: the criminally ugly, the obviously starving anorexic, an enormously obese, double amputee, etcetera. Even now I remember this one time at my grandmother's swimming club—it was me, Nate, Mom, and Nana—and suddenly I noticed this man, a regular grown-up man with the usual slightly sloppy trunks and office-white legs, only this man was covered with these large tumorlike growths. They weren't tumors, though, which I knew because later, after we had been scolded for staring at him, Nana explained that the man had a rare benign skin disorder, and then she went on and on about how it isn't someone's fault if they've got growths that look like a combination of giant acne and mushrooms sprouting all over their bodies.

It was maybe one week into the semester when a kid wearing a hugely oversized backpack did a 360 during the break between classes, swiping me with such force that I lost my balance and stumbled. Given my size, this was not a small event. Next thing I know, I had fallen smack on top of a skinny brown-haired girl of the daintily miniscule variety—mouselike bones, mouselike facial expressions—the type I could crush to death simply by sneezing. But instead of being crushed to death, she pushed me off. I wanted to apologize—and explain what had happened—but what actually came out of my mouth was something like "Er, uh."

"Are you stalking me, you big old weirdo?"

"Huh?"

"Well, just make sure you don't."

My mouth flapping open like a trap door, I just stood there, thinking that if I ever were to stalk some girl, it wouldn't be some scrawny, homely, pale, greenish-yellowish little stick of a bramblebush with flat mud-brown hair and bitten-down fingernails, not to mention a scar on her forehead that made her look like any number of homeless teen junkies. The scar, jagged and red, was so dramatic that it occurred to me that she had painted it on for effect.

"I mean it," Mouse-girl said.

Then she left and the voices (lowercase "v") took over, as they often did, howling with a ferocity that made me long for the days when I could drown my anxiety in weed without fear of doing damage to my sense organs: *You know what, Josh? You suck. You SUCK SUCK SUCK SUCK SUCK SUCK SUCK. Mouse-girl knows it. Everyone knows it. Why do you even bother? Everyone hates you and always will. Mouse-girl hates you too. Sex? Do you actually think that any girl, ever, will ever have sex with you? You'll be yanking off until the day you die.*

Hours later, after sitting in the same classes with almost all the same teachers I had my first senior year, the final bell rang. But I was too busy crying in the bathroom to hear it, missed the bus, and decided that since I couldn't bear going home and had no friends and didn't like doing anything other than eating, I would get a slice of pizza. During my second slice, Mom texted, asking me where I was, and before I could text her back, she called to make sure I wasn't dead. The town I live in, Blooming Acres, isn't all that big, and though it prides itself on being extremely diverse, liberal, leafy, organic, urbanesque, and utterly cool, it was still just a suburb, safe, quiet, boring, and small. Which is to say that at least Mom didn't hop in the old Toyota hybrid to pick me up. I walked home. All by my big-boy self. By the time I got there, Nate was sitting at the kitchen table, shoving wet cereal into his mouth straight out of its sodden yellow box.

"Impressive," I said.

"Why get a whole bowl dirty?" he said, his mouth stuffed with cinnamon Cheerios. Then he added, "I saw you talking to that weirdo."

"What weirdo?"

"That girl. The one with the scar."

"What of it?"

"Nothing. Just saw you, is all."

"Do you know her?"

"She's in my English class."

"Do you know how she got that scar?" As if I cared, which I didn't. Still, there was just something about it . . . where had I seen a scar like that before? It gave me the creeps.

"Like I'm friends with her?"

"So what's so weird about her?"

"She's just weird, is all," he said. "Says weird shit all the time. Says things like, I don't know . . ." And then, in a high whine, he imitated her: "'*Iambic pentameter.*'"

"Her saying 'iambic pentameter' in English class is weird?"

"You had to be there."

Shoving another giant spoonful of Cheerios into his mouth, he belched loudly.

"Come to think of it, the two of you would be a cute couple."

Which may have been funny in a mean way *before*, but now fell flat and sour, like a silent but deadly fart.

Also, considering that, once upon a time, I actually was part of a couple, Nate's sarcasm hurt my feelings, making me long for Sophie even more. My girlfriend, Sophie. The love of my life, Sophie. Except for one little detail, we were perfect together.

The detail being: I didn't have any idea where she was. Since waking up in the hospital with only one eye, I had been experiencing a total Sophie blackout, as black as a total eclipse of the sun. So no-longer-there was Sophie that it occurred to me that I had made her up, that she was part of the general blur of my general delusional delusion, and would have continued to doubt that she had ever existed other than as a figment of my badly engineered brain and a random girl in a random photo, if my parents didn't concur that there had indeed once been a Sophie, and now there wasn't.

The conversations went like this:

"Where's Sophie? What happened to Sophie? Why isn't she calling me back? Why can't I get in touch with her?"

"Sophie's fine."

"What happened to her? Is she all right? What are you hiding from me? Is she hurt? Is she dead?"

"Sophie's fine."

"Does she have cancer? Does she have another boyfriend? Oh my God, don't tell me that she got married. Did she get married? Is that it?

And you don't want to tell me because you think I couldn't deal with it?"

"Josh. Listen to us. Sophie's fine."

"She *is* married. She got married, didn't she? That's why I can't find her at NYU. She dropped out of college to get married."

"She's not married."

"She could be married, though. She's so beautiful, older guys were hitting on her all the time."

"She isn't married, and she's fine. We promise."

But all my efforts to contact her—email, text, phone, cell phone, letters to her parents' house, letters to her BFF—bounced back, return to sender, address unknown, eff you, Josh Cushing, you loser freak of dead animal parts, rodent waste, and bad breath.

"Then why won't she write back to me? Why won't you *tell me*?"

"Honey, sweetheart, you've got to let it go."

Let it go? Even Dr. Rose thought it was strange, or appeared to think it was strange, or at least made thoughtful *isn't this strange* faces when I told him, as I did, over and over, appointment after appointment, about Sophie's utter and complete disappearance from the face of the known planet. Because the fact of the matter was that back then—in the Great Before that was my life pre-superpowers—Sophie and I were, well, *together*. As together as any two people can be: each other's all-and-all; each other's suns; each other's oxygen, dreams, rest, and reason for being. The two of us together were everything but the main event, the ecstatic core of sexual union, which to this day I can only imagine because to this day I've never gotten any. But that was only because we were waiting for after we were married, which I know sounds stupid and retrograde and old-fashioned and Hallmark-cardy, but there you have it: we didn't want our relationship to be tawdry or easy or cheap in any way; but rather, official, real, deep, and committed.

I had met her the summer before at a summer camp in Vermont, where we were both junior counselors, only I was more junior than she was, because she was a year older than me, and about to start college at

NYU. During the summer, we would meet at the lake and kiss for hours, kissing as if we had invented it. Even though she started college in the fall and I was still in high school, I lived close enough to get into the city any time, and spent most weekends with her at her dorm. There was just something about her—something magical. She had all this great dark curly wild hair and soft-brown eyes, a slightly crooked nose, and a slightly off-balance, almost cross-eyed way of looking at you that made her look a little bit like a bird. But since my return home, I didn't even know if she knew about what had happened to me. She was like this big black, dark, deep hole in the middle of the room, the mere mention of her name threatening to swallow us all up. I kept trying and trying to remember what happened, to figure out how I lost my eye, but all I could remember for sure was Sophie's face, her face like a balloon, hovering in front of me, pale and pink, with big dark eyes.

"Don't worry about Sophie anymore; focus on yourself. Sophie's fine."

As for my eye, it was a similar story, a missing organ shrouded in mystery.

"Enough already. No one knows what happened. Even the EMS people didn't know. They found you on time, thank God, isn't that enough? It's a miracle you didn't bleed to death," explained Mom.

"DID I JAB IT OUT MYSELF? TELL ME."

"You've been through a hell of a time, son, a hell of a time, but we're going to get you through this, all of us, together," said Dad. He's an accountant/singer-songwriter-guitar player, except he hardly ever sang or played the guitar any more. He used to be thin and handsome, with thick dark hair, and he would sit on the end of my bed and play old James Taylor songs while I drifted off into nighty-night, but around the same time that I got big, he became portly, with thick gray hair and worried hands, and his guitar almost never came out of its case.

"Why can't I at least talk to her?"

"Honey." Mom was speaking in her most serious Mom voice. "Sophie was pretty freaked out about what happened to you. How you behaved, as you got sicker and sicker. We were all freaked out, and Sophie has a right to live her life without worrying about you. It's that simple. She doesn't want to be a part of your life any more. You've got to accept that."

"But she loves me!"

"Honey . . ."

"But she does!"

I was fully aware of how stupid it sounded, given that, duh, all evidence pointed to the contrary. But in my heart I knew it was true, that she loved me, and always would. She told me so herself, not once, either, but dozens, maybe even hundreds of times. What we had is the real deal. Love without time or space or beginning or end . . .

How do you explain magic? Because that's what being with Sophie was like: magical. When I was with her, I felt like I wasn't even me anymore, but some blend of the me I used to be and the me who flies in dreams. I loved everything about her: the way she smelled, the way she snorted instead of laughed, even the way she would push me off her when she didn't want to go any farther. I would practically be dying of love for her, dying of wanting, my whole body, and not just my body, but something inside me, something so deep down I didn't even know what it was, all of it melting and exploding at the same time.

But then she was gone, so gone that she may as well have been dead, with no Facebook trace, no email, no telephone, and no home telephone number, not even a telephone number for her parents' house. I even called her college roommate, whose number I still had, but she wouldn't talk to me at all, not even to say hi, or to ask how I was doing, and then her number stopped working too. And when I told Dr. Rose that the one thing I wanted was to know what had happened to Sophie, to know where she was, he just looked at me over his reading glasses and said, "In time, Josh. Be patient with yourself. Be gentle. Time . . ."

It wasn't fair, though. I had a right to know about my own history. But all Dr. Rose would do was write in his notepad and tell me that I was doing a good job.

So every day, at least once a day, it was just me, me and my thoughts and Athens, pleading, begging, praying: WHAT HAPPENED OH GOD PLEASE JUST TELL ME WHAT HAPPENED WHAT HAPPENED TO ME WHAT HAPPENED TO MY EYE WHAT HAPPENED TO SOPHIE WHAT DID I DO WHAT HAPPENED?

Except that I didn't believe in God. And God? The only thing he/ He/she/She ever said back was ⸻⸻⸻⸻⸻.

5

With my immense padding of blub-
ber, greasy black hair, overall depressed aura, and eye patch, I looked like
the chainsaw massacre psychopath bad guy in the scariest movie ever
made, so it didn't make any kind of sense that anyone would mess around
with me. And yet, just a couple of weeks after I tumbled into Mouse-
girl, I heard my name being called, turned, and saw this homely little
dude pointing at me and saying, "Hey, yo there, Super-butt. Yeah, *you.*
Think you can save my ass from flunking my geometry quiz?"

On either side of him were two more of his kind: small, geeky, un-
pretty, and undersized, dressed in nearly identical black nouveaux goth
T-shirts, black jeans, and floppy black canvas shoes. The way they
buzzed frantically around me reminded me of insects.

"Go away," I said.

They didn't. Instead, they circled me, as if in an effort to corral me against the lockers. It occurred to me that I could take them out with a single well-aimed punch, but, sadly, violence had never been my forte. Also, I didn't want to be sent back to the slammer. So I made a calculated decision to give them the meanest, baddest-ass glower I could. I glowered so hard my face hurt.

It didn't work.

"Hey man, will you change my water into wine?"

"What I want to know is: if you're so special, why are you such a loser?"

"Little dandelions," I said, which didn't make much sense but was the best insult I could come up with. It didn't, however, stop the first of this trio of comedians from saying, "Why did the cyclops close his school?"

Ignoring the voices in my head as best I could, I turned to go. But the ugly little guy had other plans, coming so close that I could smell the bacon and peanut butter on his breath and see the detailed scroll-work of his braces.

"Because he only had one pupil," he answered. "Get it?"

I wanted to punch his lights out.

Eventually, I figured that he was acting on a dare—a dare that he would brag about to all two of his crew of two—and was, perhaps, clenching with every fiber in his nether-muscles to keep from peeing in his pants. But at the time, I just stared at his very pale white skin.

"Later."

"Don't you want to hear the song?"

"No."

"You sure?"

"Yup."

"But we wrote it special."

"You don't hear good, do you?"

Too late: they were singing. The song was short but catchy:

Why do you ask: why why why?
Is it because of my one blue eye?
Perhaps I poked it out myself
And lost it up upon the shelf.
I flew above the world to find
That I'd gone and lost my mind.

"Lame" is what I finally managed to say, but by then the other two had joined in, jumping and swaggering in a little circle dance around me, making it difficult for me to get past them without smacking them silly. Dr. Rose had taken me through what he called "decompression exercises" in which I practiced breathing deeply while intoning the words "they can't hurt me, they can't hurt me" inside my mind. The idea was to avoid the regret, shame, and guilt that any acting out, or act of destruction, would invariably cause me. The exercise was mainly meant to help me during times of internal, rather than external, stress, during times when the voices got too chatty, or my own not-knowing-what-happened became too miserable for me to bear. Neither one of us had anticipated that I would be the object of harassment via insect posse.

The first bell rang, signaling the start of third period, precalc. with Mr. Watson—the hardest hard-ass at Western High. The kind who threw chalk at you if he thought you weren't paying attention, and took points off for the most minor of minor infractions.

Meantime, a small crowd had gathered. Just what I fucking needed.

"Hit 'em," someone said.

"Come on, you can do it," a second person said.

"What a bunch of cockroaches."

"We're on your side, man."

"Teach 'em a lesson."

It occurred to me then that perhaps Dr. Rose was wrong: that rather than feeling some sense of regret or defeat, nothing would feel better than using my great girth for a small act of violence in the cause of justice. Isn't that what the good guys always did, the cops, the cowboys, the heroes of World War II? I could already feel the sweet satisfaction of cartilage crunching beneath my knuckles, when, from the crowd, Mouse-girl stepped forward.

"Y'all are just a bunch of underaged brats," she said. "Scat."

And with that, the insects scrammed, one after the other, laughing. The little audience that had gathered to see the fight went away too, leaving just the two of us, me and Mouse-girl, standing together in the hall under the green buzzing glow of the fluorescent lights.

"What the?" I finally stammered, eloquent as always.

Mouse-girl looked at me with an expression that made my blood boil: a combination of pity and disdain, with an overlay of boredom.

My one eyeball twitched. Then, a miracle: I strung an entire coherent sentence together. "Why'd you do that? I don't need your help."

"Yeah," she said, apparently having decided that our staring contest had gotten old, drawing the one word out to two long syllables— *yee-eeh*—like if she couldn't win the staring contest, at least she would win the verbal-intonation one.

"I was about to take them out."

"Uh huh."

"And another thing. What's your problem?"

"What's *your* problem? Dumbass."

"Where'd you learn to talk like that?"

"Gotta go," she said, and go she did, shooting down the hall like a bullet.

I hated her. I hated her even worse than I hated Susan at TITSS, because at least Susan had an excuse, namely that she was a flat-out crazy nuts loony psycho. Whereas Mouse-girl: who did she think she was? Had she *drawn* that scar on for extra effect? Which is exactly what I was going to accuse her of, except that I was so fat that my running was more like plodding with wet shoes in wet sand. Pathetic. Especially considering that, once upon a time, I was the best runner that Western High had ever seen, and our coach—Coach Dupe—was talking about all the scholarships that were within my reach. Now I couldn't even catch up with a girl the size of a large squirrel.

Gasping from my herculean effort, I heard an announcement crackle over the PA system: "Attention students! By now everyone seems to be settling in again, and we're off to a great start!"

It had been a big decision, whether to send me back to Western High, or some other, special, private school for wackos. But after all the dough my parents had already shelled out on my treatment, and all the dough that was going to Dr. Rose, they just couldn't afford it. Plus I figured that even if they were swimming in money, going back to Western wasn't as bad as going to Camberville Academy, where you can't get in at all unless you demonstrate a marked inability to understand nothing about nothing under all circumstances always. Being at Western was like déjà vu every day, though, weird to be back in the classes I'd already taken but couldn't remember. Like chemistry? I used to love chemistry. I used to love thinking about atomic structure, the periodic table, molecules, compounds, quantum numbers. Now it was just one big so-what. Worse, they put me back in Mrs. Garret's class. I liked Mrs. Garret, but she stood over me, hovering like a second mom.

The voice over the PA continued: "And as you know, homecoming is next Friday! That's right—just a week away! Tickets for the homecoming dance are available through the front office. Go, Huskies!"

What happened to my *eye*? But all I remembered was this awful feeling of being trapped, like when you're having a bad dream and you can't wake up and even though you know you're sleeping, after a while you're convinced that it's really happening. This awful feeling of all the walls pushing in on me. A kind of queasiness in my bones. And then there it was: the hole in my face, the dent where my right eye used to be. The black eye patch. I looked *ridiculous*. Like it was Halloween every day of the week, with just a sewed-up socket, like an asshole, wrinkled and pink and ugly, where my eye used to be. The doctors wanted to wait for it to heal more before I was fitted for a glass eye.

When I got to class, Mr. Watson threw some chalk my way but it missed and hit the wall. As I shuffled to my seat, he launched into yet another lecture about starting the semester off on the right foot and showing up on time and not disrupting and remembering to study, math is math, you can't let it slide like some of those other subjects where you can catch up from behind, blah blah, and then I stopped listening.

Lunch was macaroni and cheese and baked chicken cardboard. I sat by myself. As I got up to clear my tray, I noticed Mouse-girl, also eating by herself. She was watching me, like a scientist observing a bug.

6

In early October, during one of the regular, interminable, no-one-is-sharing silences that happened at TITSS, Fleur turned brightly to me and said, "How about you, Josh?"

"Don't you mean *Satan*?" Susan snorted.

"Not now, Susan," Fleur said.

But Susan, lost in her own fumes, continued anyway. "Because he's anti-God," she snorted. "Plus he smells like dog-doo."

It was true that I wasn't newly showered, but on the other hand, I was pretty sure there weren't any dog excretions on me. But because I'd come late and the only place left was next to her, Susan probably could smell my other odors, including my sour breath, my clammy pits, my even clammier palms.

"If you'd like to share, that's fine, too, Susan," Fleur said in her calm, professional voice. "But right now I'm asking Josh. How about it, Josh? You haven't shared for a while."

From Susan came rapid-fire rat-a-tat-tat *snaps* as she pulled on the collection of blue and red rubber bands she wore around her wrist. Irritating, but who among us didn't understand that there's nothing like a sharp stab of intense pain to shake you out of being dead inside?

"Josh?"

All eyes were on me as I shifted my weight, as if I could get comfortable just by finding the right balance between right and left butt flanks. The chairs were hard and metal, designed to send you to the chiropractor. It had been a couple of weeks since the Mouse-girl versus the insects incident, but they had come at me a second and then a third time, and even though each subsequent time was a kind of repeat—with other kids stopping to tell me that they were on my side and calling the insects fagbites and dweebs and hemorrhoids—I felt embarrassed by the whole deal, itchy, like I had an internal rash. If Mom found out about these three little dweebs, it would be all over for me, and I might as well let her choose my clothes, give me my baths, and tuck me in at night.

Next to me, Susan began to peel the skin off her perfectly formed chapped lips.

"Josh?" Fleur tried again.

"What?"

"Would you like to share? Anything going on?"

"Okay," I said, not because I meant it but because it seemed better to say something than to say nothing while Susan worked on turning her lips into a bloody smear. "I started sleeping with Athens again."

What I didn't say was that even with Athens curled up in my arms, I couldn't really sleep. It was more like I'd lie awake, staring at the ceiling, obsessing about Sophie, trying and failing to will myself into remembering what happened to my eye, and then, right around the time it started getting light, I'd lose track of things, and blink out.

"Athens?" Fleur prompted.

"My dog," I explained. "Stuffed dog. A stuffed animal, I mean. He talks to me. Not really. I mean, it's not like I'm hearing voices. Not *voices* voices. I mean, I have them too, but I know that they're coming from inside my mind. Sometimes they can be kind of loud though. But Athens, he's not alive. I mean, he's not a dead dog who's been stuffed. Which would be disgusting. I mean, we already have a dog. An alive one. The kind that does nothing all day but sniff your crotch. He's a yellow lab."

Poor Buster: he was so old that he could barely walk, so arthritic that when he peed he couldn't even bother to lift his leg.

"His name is Buster," I said, kicking off my shoes—the same pair of boat shoes I had worn in the nuthouse once it was determined that I could wear shoes again just so long as they didn't have shoelaces, because as everyone knows, if you have enough shoelaces, you can hang yourself with them, which you can't, not really, because they're not strong enough. "Buster is our dog," I continued. "Our real dog, that is."

"Jesus Christ, blubber-head," Susan said under her breath. All around me, kids began to pull out their cigarettes, as if they could already smell the heavenly smell of decaying lungs and nicotine laced smoke. But I was on a tear. A tear! *Go Josh go you're almost there you're going to win you've got it go go go go!*

"And also, my dad won't eat meat anymore. He thinks he's going to get cancer, that meat gives you cancer, that he has to eat mainly vegetables or he'll get sick and die."

By now it was like my mouth had a separate motor attached to it and couldn't stop.

"And also, at school, there's this girl. I feel like she's just kind of always *there*. As in, every time I turn around, she's watching me."

"Do we have to listen to this cow plop horse manure?" interrupted Susan, jumping to her feet with such fury that it was as if an electric wire had been run through her body.

"Sit down," said Fleur.

"But don't you see?" Susan continued as if Fleur weren't even there.

"He's fooling you. He's fooling all of you. He thinks he's got MAGIC POWERS. He's dangerous. He wants to be my boyfriend."

"Sit down or I'll have to ask you to leave the meeting," said Fleur.

"No need," Susan yelled as she pulled out a cigarette, lit up, and flicked the lit cig into the air, where it hovered for a nanosecond as if it had wings of its own before dropping directly onto the big top jutting-out bone of my non-covered-by-my-boat-shoe right foot, where, when all was said and done, it left a nice open bloody blister. So utterly freaked out was my mother when, later, she noticed my injured foot that she called the director of the organization that ran the TITSS meetings and all but threatened to sue.

Two days later, during dinner stir-fry with stir-fried tofu and stir-fried vegetables and not one lick of anything edible, Mom got up to answer the phone, said "uh huh, uh huh" into the mouthpiece a few times, nodded and shook her head, hung up, and returned to the table, where she said, "That was Mrs. Garret."

"Mrs. Garret, my chemistry teacher?"

"The very one."

"What? I fucked up one of my quizzes?"

"I wish you wouldn't talk like that, Josh," Dad said. "Especially to your mother."

"She didn't say anything about your schoolwork," Mom said. "Josh, what's this about some boys at school harassing you?" I must have made a face that was like *Holy hell bite me* because she said, "This is serious, Josh. Mrs. Garret says that there are some boys who follow you around school making up songs about you. Is this true?" I just looked at her like *Gee, oops.* "What on earth? You've got to let us know about things like that, honey. Or if not me and Dad, someone else: Dr. Rose, at the very least. You just don't think things through, sometimes. And worse, you shut us out, me and Dad, both, and after all we've been through—together, as a family—well, that's just not fair, Josh."

It was Nate, of all people, who came to my rescue. "It's just a bunch of freshmen idiots, Mom."

"What?"

"Complete morons. No one pays any attention to them. Everyone's like: what a bunch of little creeps. These kids are immature piss bubbles, is all it is."

"Is all? Is all? Good God, Nate, what kind of attitude is that? For one thing, bullying is bullying. And for another, it happens to be against the law."

"What are you looking at me for? I didn't fucking do anything."

"I said don't talk to your mother like that," said Dad.

"You told *Josh* not to talk to Mom like that. Not me."

The joke fell flat though. Dad turned white with anger. "But you knew about it. What were you thinking? Why didn't you say something?"

"Because I didn't, okay? Because maybe I thought there was enough drama around here to begin with? Because I'm *done.*"

He stormed out of the room. The moments clicked by. I sat there looking at my plate until I figured that it was time for me to take my exit as well, and got up to clear. Except it was already too late.

"Do you know who these boys are, Josh?" Mom asked.

"I mean, not their names."

"But you could identify them?" said Dad.

"I guess."

"How many people are we talking about here?" said Mom.

"Three."

"Three? You sure there are three? Not four? Not five?"

"I think I can count, Mom."

"Do you think they're going to do it again?"

"No clue."

"Are you sure?"

"Huh?"

"How many times have they done it so far, Josh? Once? Twice? More than that?" asked Mom.

"Don't know. I try not to pay attention."

"You don't have *any* idea? How is that possible?" said Dad.

I shrugged.

"Guess what?" Mom said. "I'm a lawyer. I know the law. And this is harassment, and it's against the law." She wore her graying hair very short, like a boy's, and flowing flowery dresses. I couldn't tell whether she was pretty, or ever had been.

"Got it."

"I'm not sure you do, Josh—are you listening to me, Josh? If this goes on much longer, as in even one more time, I'm going to get the principal involved. And if she can't help, then I'll go to local enforcement, because it's worse than indecent, Josh, this kind of harassment. I want to put a stop to it before . . ."

She didn't say it, but she didn't have to. I knew exactly what she meant.

7

After the dual incidents of the cigarette-on-foot-burn followed by the Mom-and-Dad-finding-out-about-the-insects, I decided that the best way to handle my parents' newly ramped-up urge to watch my every move like I was a bug under a microscope was by acting like any regular normal high school student without a care in the world other than getting into the college of his choice.

In other words, I decided to go to the homecoming game.

Mom was thrilled. "Wonderful!" she exhaled. "It will be so good for you to go out there and socialize, to mix it up again with your own peer group."

"Right."

"It'll be fun!"

For just long enough for me to forget about my blubber, my misfiring neurons, and my status as the most untouchable human being in all of Western High's robust outcast caste, I let myself sink into a fantasy of sitting on the stands on a cool evening and rooting for the Huskies, THE HOWLIN' HUSKIES, HEAR US HOWL! *All I'll have to do is sit there and watch the game*, I thought. *It'll be fine.*

Dad refined the plan by offering up Nate as my babysitter. "He can drive," he said. "And with the two of you together, you won't have to feel self-conscious."

"Have you asked Nate?"

"Of course I've asked Nate!" Dad said.

"And?"

"He thought it was a swell idea."

Since Nate's never thought anything was a swell idea that didn't include something special for Nate—a ski trip, say, or Yankees tickets— I knew right away that Nate had been strong-armed into the deal. Even so, I didn't expect him to ditch me as soon as we pulled into Western High's parking lot.

"Later, dude," he said as the car doors thumped shut behind us.

It was a warm night—almost as warm as summer—with girls in skirts and guys in T-shirts sporting the names of their favorite rock groups. I myself was attractively arrayed in size huge baggy plaid beach-dude shorts, a Rutgers size ginormous T-shirt, and completing the fashion look, size 12 flip-flops, which, though accommodating the burned top half of my right foot, made loud slapping noises as I ascended the aluminum stairs of the bleachers. But aside from the usual glance-and-look-away stares, no one paid any attention to me one way or another. It was like I was a human force field, pushing others of my species as far away from me as possible.

In front of the bleachers, the cheerleaders were prancing and dancing in their dark-green-and-yellow uniforms, shaking their pom-poms and grinning like their faces didn't know any better, and as the team ran out onto the field, everyone got on their feet to cheer. Even when I was all-state, with a school record for the 5k, the best I got, in terms of high school fame, was the occasional photo on the back page of the school newspaper. Cheerleaders or crowds? Not so much.

A few moments after the game began, someone lobbed a half-eaten wiener my way, hitting me in the back of the neck. I turned and saw the insects.

Really? I thought. And then: *That's it.* And then: *What was I thinking?* Time to go home, I realized, which unfortunately meant walking home, which I really wasn't in the mood for, not in flip-flops. *Slap, slap, slap,* they announced as I descended the metal steps, when some kid I had never seen before said, "It's all right, man. Ignore those creeps."

I appreciated it, I really did, but it was too late: I didn't even like football, never had. It's just one of those things you do in high school: you go to football games, you go to parties, and even if you're bored to death, you hang out.

"Thanks," I said but kept going, *slap, slap, slap, thud, thud, thud,* my vast weight shaking the stands, until I was on the very last step, where, just my luck, I stumbled, tripped, caught myself, but nevertheless brushed up against, fuck me, Mouse-girl.

She looked her usual nondescript mouse-self, in cut-off jeans and a T-shirt emblazoned with the words "Roll Tide."

"Get away from me," she said.

"It was an accident, okay? Sorry."

"Are you *following* me?"

"Isn't it the other way around?"

"What the hell?" A second later, she was walking away from me hyperfast, as if she thought I was planning on killing her.

Meanwhile, my voices had started up again, babbling on about going to the senior prom next spring. *You can take Mommy, Mommy would love to be your date, she'll get all dressed up and let you kiss her but not that way you silly boy you really are a sick sicko aren't you senior prom, sure, you'll go to the senior prom, that sounds just dandy dandy dandy!*

Stupid voices.

Shut up, voices.

Even Mouse-girl is on to you. Even she knows how badly you suck. Look at her running away from you.

But I wouldn't have it. It was too absurd. She was—what? Five foot zero inches? Five foot one? Without really thinking it through, I decided to go after her, to explain, to set the record straight.

An aeon later, panting for breath, I was within earshot of her. I could see the way her shoulder blades twitched under her shirt. Summoning as much volume as I could muster, I pleaded: "Can (*pant pant*) I (*hhhh*) ask (*wheeze*) you (*gasp*) something?"

"Go away."

"Just hold (*hhhwheeze*) up a minute."

"You don't hear real good, do you?"

"Please?" (*Cough hack wheeze pant cough.*)

"Leave me alone!"

I'd followed her through the parking lot, past Dad's car, and to the edge of the woods when I felt a quick, fierce, searing pain in my left foot, and fell with a heavy thud. My foot hurt so badly I actually heard myself howling, and when I say "heard myself," what I mean is that I didn't even know that it was me making all that noise until I heard the sound coming back at me. Which may or may not have been one of the many side effects of my meds. In any event, as I righted myself, I heard a second howl, this time from the stands behind me: HOWLING HUSKIES HEAR US HOWL! It all mixed together in my mind, like the ocean had escaped its deep plunging beds and taken up residency in my skull.

"Are you all right?"

Mouse-girl was standing a few feet from me, her white face a blank. Behind us, the crowd was still doing its stomp-and-cheer-and-roar thing. I waited for my breathing to return to something like normal.

"I think so."

"You're not going to pull anything, are you?"

"Like what, exactly?"

"Like jump up and grab me."

"*What?*" What with my daily dose of antipsychotics, my missing eyeball, my missing girlfriend, and my voices, I knew that I didn't exactly have it all together. Still, I had no clue what she could possibly have been talking about. I could barely walk, let alone jump.

"Kids in this town are mean as snakes. Bunch of hussy skank bitches talking about me—to my face—like I'm toe lint."

As she began to walk away again, I said, "Wait! I'm bleeding like a slaughtered cow."

All right, I wasn't bleeding like a slaughtered cow. I was, however, bleeding—the scab on my foot had opened up, and my toes were scraped. My palms, where I'd caught myself, were raw and painful, too.

"I doubt you'll bleed to death," Mouse-girl said, turning to look at me.

"It hurts."

"Boo-hoo. You took a little tumble. I'm supposed to feel sorry for you?"

"Look," I finally said after trying and then failing to piece together some semblance of a comeback. "I'm sorry if I scared you. But I just want to ask you a question. Just one small question."

She looked at me like perhaps I was covered in green Play-Doh. But at last she relented, crossed her arms, and said, "What?"

"Who *are* you?"

"What's it to you?"

"It's just," I said as I tried to get a grip on the slipperiness of this interchange. "It's like every time I look up, there you are. Like you're doing a science report on me. I mean, I know I'm not real pretty . . ." But then I got fixated on that scar of hers, and ran out of words.

"So what if you don't look like a movie star? Who cares? There's this kid in my English class who looks just like you, only thin, and he seems to think that he's a god."

"My brother," I said.

"Huh?"

"Big feet, right? Like size 12?"

"You are freaking me out."

"Why? My brother has big feet."

"Why are we talking about your brother? Who cares about your brother?"

"But you said—" But I didn't really know what she'd said, and anyway, she had turned and was off again.

"Hold on! Wait up!" I said as I scrambled up after her, touching her lightly by her elbow. She turned to face me. It was then that I noticed her eyes, dark green, sparkling, inquisitive, innocent, sharp. And above them, that nasty scar, pink and rubbery, snaking up into her hairline.

"My brother, Nate," I said. "He must have told you all about me."

"One, I don't know anyone named Nate, although there is this kid in my English class named Nathan, and okay, I see. He's your brother. Got it. On the other hand, huh? I've never talked to him."

"You're telling me that you don't know about my, er, adventures?"

"What, you've been to Disneyland?"

"In a manner of speaking, I guess you could say."

"Relevance?"

"I was being sardonic. Ironic. Sarcastic. I didn't go to Disneyland."

"They why did you say you did?"

Scouts honor, I had never had a conversation like that with anyone, anywhere. Not even in the loony bin, where people were pretty raw. So it was something of a minor miracle when, after I begged for a little while, Mouse-girl allowed me to explain one or two particulars about my life as I had heretofore lived it, such as the fact that I'd been bonkers. And then, when I was all done explaining, she turned to me, let out a big sigh, and said, "Wow. That must have totally sucked."

"Kind of."

"Probably still sucks, huh?"

"Kind of."

"And people," she said. "They can just be such suckheads."

We began to walk. After a little while I realized that I was breathing normally again, and she didn't seem scared.

"What's your name?"

"Elizabeth," she said. "Elizabeth Rinaldi."

"Italian?"

"Scots-Irish-Italian-Romanian-Cajun-French," she said.

"I'm Josh."

"I know."

"How do you know?"

"I've heard people say, *Hey, Josh.* Or: *Leave Josh alone, idiots.* You know, with that little fan club of yours."

"Ah, yes. The fans. I have to beat them off with a stick."

"So you've spent some real quality time in hospitals, huh?"

"You could say that."

"I did say that," she said.

8

When I first woke up in the hospital, I didn't feel like a person at all, let alone a person who goes by the tag of "Josh Cushing," but more like a blob—a blob on a bed. I had no clue where I was. Sound came to me as though I was in a tunnel. My eyes felt like they had been glued together with honey.

There was a slight rustling noise, and then a woman's face hovered into view, more like an apparition, a ghost version of a face. Each feature registered separately: nose, mouth, chin, eyebrows, but it didn't add up to *face*. Watery green ovals for eyes; short brown straw for hair; rubbery brown-pink skin around teeth that I finally realized were lips.

"Where am I?"

"Josh?"

"Who are you?"

"Josh! Thank God."

"What's on my face?"

"I'll be right back," she said.

My throat was burning. My mouth was dry. My tongue felt like it was made of rope. When I tried to get up, I couldn't. It was as if I had been cemented onto the bed.

Above me, a TV hung suspended in the corner. Light slanted in through dirty gray windows. Where my left eye should have been, there was nothing but a dull, throbbing pain.

"WHERE AM I!?" I screamed.

Except it didn't come out that way. Instead, the words were dry, like dead dry leaves in my dry-as-sand mouth: a hoarse whisper.

The woman returned. Something about her reminded me of something, or of someone, or perhaps a place—of certain smells, of a certain feeling of when I was little, running, running—and of warm bath water. Of powder. Of leather: baseball mitts. Dress shoes. I noticed that her green, mild, milky eyes were shiny with tears. Behind her was a woman wearing light-blue pajamas. She was young. Black straight hair. Bead-black eyes. Skin as smooth as the inside of seashells. She wore a large, abstract necklace around her neck, with two facing discs. No, not pajamas: scrubs. Not a necklace: a stethoscope. Her eyes scanned something on the wall, then she lowered herself onto the side of my bed.

"I'm Dr. Chang," she said, shining a bright light into my unbandaged eye. "This won't take long. Do you know who you are? Can you tell me?"

"Who are you?"

"I'm a doctor here. Can you tell me who *you* are?"

"I'm Josh?" I croaked, vaguely remembering that the other woman had called me that. The doctor nodded, so I figured that I got it right. Gold star for me.

"Do you know where you are?"

But I had already forgotten my name, and as for where I was—I guess I wouldn't be getting that gold star after all. And that's because . . .

"Josh?" said the first woman, whoever she was. "Josh?"

She was talking to me.

"What?"

"Do you know who you are?"

The words didn't even make sense. Nothing did. Except one thing: Sophie. Because just like that, Sophie—the sound of her, the smell of her, the feel of her—came rushing back to me. Along with this terrible queasy feeling that something had happened—something bad—and that something had to do with Sophie. Panic poured into me, only I didn't know it was panic. I didn't even know what panic was, or who I was, or what I was doing, there in that bed, in that place, in that strange spinning room . . .

"Where's Sophie?" I said, but even as I said it, I wasn't sure what I meant, just that the words had to come out. "Where's Sophie? What have you done with Sophie?"

"Sweetheart . . ."

"Sophie," I said with the last of my breath, because truthfully, I hadn't exactly been speaking, in words, at all. It was more like I had managed to get a series of sounds out, of syllables, of terrified grunts and squawks.

"Okay, then," the doctor said, ignoring my not-words as she held my eye open with one hand while with the other she beamed a light into it. "You've had an accident. I just need to look into your eye for a few more seconds, hold on for me, okay, looks good." It was when she put the light down that I realized that, though I wanted to, I couldn't talk no matter what: not with a towel in my throat.

"Do you want something to drink?"

I nodded, desperate, while she indicated to the other woman standing there—the one with the liquid green eyes and sad, tired posture—to bring me some water. Then she was holding the water under my chin, directing a straw into my mouth. "That's it," she murmured as tears ran down her face. Then, glancing over at the doctor, she said, "I don't think he knows who I am."

"Give him a few moments. Let the fog clear."

"Do you know who I am, Josh?"

I didn't. Still, there was something about her—the weight of her. Her rumpled sweatshirt. The sound of her voice.

"Josh?"

"Mrs. Garret?"

"Honey?"

"Did the lab explode?" I say, proud of myself for having finally recognized her. "Did I get acid in my eye?"

"We thought we'd lost you," she said.

"Am I in the hospital?" But it was impossible, with the towel down my throat, and the throbbing pain in my eye and the cement where my bones used to be. My words weren't words, but hoarse, cough-like croaks.

"It's hard for you to talk because you have a breathing tube down your throat," she said.

"What's wrong with my *eye*?" I said, and just like that, I returned to my body, to being Josh Cushing, seventeen years old, training for All-County, but somehow in a hospital with my AP chemistry teacher, a doctor, and a thick wad of bandaging over my left eye.

"Was I in a car crash?" I rasped.

"No, sweetie."

"Did Sophie die?"

"You're in a hospital, Josh." This time, it was the doctor, talking in a smooth, controlled voice. "You've been here about a week. We've medicated you, put you in a kind of semi-sleep. Because you lost a lot of blood. You lost your eye."

"I lost my eye." I had no clue what that meant.

"You've been very, very sick."

"No." It was the only sound I was able to utter, and I heard it over and over, inside my mind where it screamed: *NO NO NO NO NO NO NO!*

"Josh," the doctor finally said. "You've had what's called a schizophrenic break. You weren't in your right mind."

Later, I would think of crazy people, empty-eyed ghoulish men and women in restraints, tied into their beds, drooling. What I thought then was *What the . . . ?*

"You only have one eye. The other one is gone—it was damaged beyond repair . . ."

And since that day to this, I haven't been able to find out a single other thing about what happened to me, back then, during my special gig—about how I lost my eye, about where Sophie is, about what I did or didn't do. My memory is a black wash, and though Dr. Rose assures me that with time things may come back to me, there's no guarantee. The truth is, I don't even remember much of what it was like when I thought I was—well, whatever I thought I was—just glimmers, bits and pieces, like snatches of conversation that you hear but don't hear as you pass kids talking at their lockers. It's like I was in a coma, but not, because in a coma you may as well be in the deep freeze, with nothing other than a few vital organs up and running, and the mind, the personality, the you within the you of you, a blank, like what you were before you were born. When I was little and asked about that, about who I was before I was born, Mom and Dad always said the same thing: "You were a wish we wished for." That was nice, as far as it went, but it didn't answer the question. Nor did what they told me when I was finally well enough to get out of the hospital, finally well enough to eat and drink and poop without help, to make sense of spoken language, and to speak with some degree of competence. It was like learning a foreign language, except of course, I already knew it. *Blue* is the color of the sky on a clear summer day; *dog* is that smelly furry thing that licks you with his tongue; *hug* is a person putting their arms around you and squeezing but not squeezing so hard it hurts; *Josh* is short for *Joshua Cushing*, the older of the two Cushing boys, you've heard of him, haven't you . . . ? Such a bright boy, so gifted, and such an athlete, and then one day, well, it could happen to anyone, such a tragedy, he starts ranting and raving—some people think he poked his own eye out—his poor parents, can you only imagine how frantic with worry they must have been?

I didn't tell everything to Elizabeth, not that night, anyway, but I did tell her a lot, so much so that I didn't even notice that the game was over until I got home and found that Dad's car was already in the driveway.

As I walked up the front steps, I heard Nate going head-to-head with Mom and Dad.

"What do you mean he didn't stay for the game? Why didn't you go after him?"

"But Mom! What was I supposed to do? Drag him back?"

"I don't know! You could have done *something*. Gotten some of your teammates to join you. Been *nicer* to him. Why are you so awful to your brother? What? You think I don't know?"

"Don't know what, Mom? What are you talking about?"

"The awful way you treat him, now that he's back. How could you have just left him there to fend for himself, on the bleachers? You know how hard it is for him to socialize. How hard it is for him to do *anything*."

"So I went to talk to my friends. Since when is that a crime?"

"You *know* how fragile he is, Nate! The least you could do is try. But no. Take the lazy man's way out. You always have."

"Fragile? Right. Dude weighs about three hundred pounds."

"What's *wrong* with you, Nate?"

"I'm out of here."

"That's right," Mom screamed after him. "Just walk away. Just don't care. That's always been the way you've dealt with things, just walking away from them. You're just plain selfish, is what you are."

In front of me, my little brother hurtled himself through the door, slamming it behind him. A moment later, I watched him striding across the lawn and then jogging up the street. He hadn't even seen me.

9

You know what's funny? For most of my life, I just kind of skated through everything. My friends were my friends. Occasionally a girl would like me or I'd like a girl and we would pass notes in class or meet at the big oak tree at middle school or later, in high school, at Dunkin' Donuts or the Skinny Deli or in the park. I played sports, got invited to birthday parties, tossed a Frisbee around with my friends, or with Nate. I never really thought about the geeks or the losers or funny-looking girls who never got asked to the prom or gay goths or those fat kids with asthma and bad haircuts. They just weren't part of my world. Mom was Mom, Dad was Dad, and Nate was the bratty kid he had always been: when he really got on my nerves I would take a swipe at him, just the usual brother-on-brother wrestling-around-on-the-carpet stuff. I never even got mad at him, not really, not in any serious way, except this one time when he kept barging into my room when I was trying to study and I had to threaten to bash his head against the wall to get him to stop. By the time I was in high school I was so big that when he got on my nerves or started to pick a fight, all I would have to do was lift him up and put him somewhere else. Once when he was driving me bonkers, I picked him up and put him on the toilet and closed the door to the bathroom and wouldn't let him out until he promised to call me "Sir" for a week. Then he caught up with me, size-wise, but even so, I was still the big brother, the more powerful of the two of us. But all that changed, along with everything else, when I came back home after my time on planet fruitcake, sentenced to having a second senior year. Nate had meantime become like me but better, tall and athletic and so unselfconsciously popular and confident that even the most unreachable girls gazed at him with longing.

Given that Nate and I had become experts at ignoring each other, it came as a bit of a surprise when, one morning before first period, he turned to me and said, "It must bite being you."

"Yeah, well."

My brother looked down at his black low-rise Converse sneakers that made his feet look even bigger than they were. The rims around his eyes were going pink, like he was about to cry.

"What is it, Nate?"

"I just . . ."

"What?"

"I just feel so bad for you. It isn't your fault, what happened . . ."

"It isn't your fault either."

"It's just—" But he stopped there, unable or unwilling to say out loud what we were both thinking about, namely, that upon his return the night before, Mom, who'd been waiting up for him, had given him a second tongue-lashing.

"Sorry I ditched you like that," he said.

"Sorry Mom lit into you like that."

"I don't know, man," he said, and then, as the warning bell shrieked, he slammed his locker closed and took off down the corridor.

I wanted to cry. Instead, I went into the bathroom and punched the mirror so hard it cracked, which was a seriously stupid idea, given that my hand still hurt from my recent tumble. And then, of course, I was once again late for math class, where I once again got a piece of chalk thrown my way, and Mr. Watson once again made noises about not disrupting his class and rules are rules, they're there for a reason, no exceptions, blah blah blah . . .

My hand was still hurting when, at lunch, Elizabeth slid herself next to me and her tray next to mine like she and I had been lunching à la besties since we were born. On her plate was what was supposed to have been a submarine sandwich but was more like a giant roll with a shaving of meat in the middle. I had opted for the vegetarian option—in this case, flaccid spaghetti covered with watery red slime.

"So Nathan's your brother," she said, all matter-of-fact.

"Yup. Only everyone calls him Nate."

"Not Mrs. Darling. She calls everyone by their full name. *Lucille. Maxwell. Benjamin. Elizabeth.* Except of course I'm already *Elizabeth.* Mama always said that she gave me a beautiful name for a reason and she didn't want it shortened to Betsy or Liz."

"Got it," I said.

"Nathan's kind of, I don't know. Not real interested in the subtleties and grandeur of the great works of literature."

"That would be my brother."

"And you meant it when you told me that you spent some time on a cruise to candy-land?"

"Unfortunately, I cannot tell a lie."

"And now you're back to normal."

"With the help of pharmaceuticals."

"I had this friend once," she said, taking a bite from her giant sandwich. "From home. I mean, not a good friend, not a best friend, or anything like that, but this girl, Nina was her name, she was real real sweet. Then, at the beginning of eleventh grade, she starts getting weirder and weirder, and the next thing I know, it was going around school that she'd flipped out and her parents had had to put her in the hospital, I don't know exactly. Anyway, it was sad."

"What happened to her? Is she okay?"

"I don't know," Elizabeth said. "We moved."

"After junior year? That's cruel."

"Well, we moved anyway."

"Why?"

"Mama wanted to. She said it would be better for both of us, that we'd have better opportunities here."

"So you just up and moved . . . to *New Jersey*?"

She gave me a palms-up-shrug-bored-who-knows look. I tried not to stare at her scar. "It's complicated."

"Can't be any more complicated than being off your nut."

"You'd think."

Her words hung in the air, so resonant that I could almost see them. It was suddenly obvious that she had a story, too.

"How'd you get that?" I said, pointing at her scar, and then, immediately, regretting my words. Because, first: who gave me permission to go poking around in her business? And, second: it filled me with anxiety, that scar, reminding me of something that I couldn't name. And third: well, there was no third, not exactly, except that it made me sad. I mean, I may have been a big fat sweaty one-eyed weirdo, but, as it had been pointed out to me innumerable times, I would soon have two eyes, and I could lose the weight if I tried, whereas Elizabeth was a girl, and no amount of aerobic exercise or non-cheeseburger diet would erase that mark on her forehead.

"Like I said, it's complicated."

"Look—" I started to say, about to launch into a routine about how my mom was driving me even crazier than I had been before, when suddenly she turned to me, and went pink.

"There was this other thing, too," she said quickly.

"Whatever it was," I said, intending to be funny but aware, even as the words came out of my mouth, that I wasn't, "it can't be as bad as being a teenage schizophrenic, which is what I technically am."

Hunkering down and lowering her voice, as if the whole world, or at least that little slice of it represented by the inmates of Western High, were desperate to overhear our conversation, she said, "If I tell you, you have to promise never, and I mean never ever, to tell another soul. Not your brother. Not your parents. Not your priest—"

"Rabbi," I corrected.

"Not no one. Do you understand me?"

"I understand."

"Do you promise?"

"Do I have a choice?"

"This is serious," she hissed. "Life or death serious. Do you promise, or not?"

"Fine. Okay. I get it." And I did, and that was because I knew, at that very moment, that Elizabeth wasn't capable of mincing words, prevarication, or lying, that she was—is—the most trustworthy person I would ever know. How I knew this I can't say except to say that my guts knew it first, and then my brain, and then my mouth. And we had only been friends, if that's what we were, for half a day.

"And by the way," she said, "you may be a psycho-whatever-you-call-it, but you don't act any dumber than most kids around here."

"Thanks. I love compliments."

"I mean, some of these kids, even in the AP classes, they talk like—*morons*. Obsessed about the dumbest things."

"I guess."

"But seriously, if I'm going to tell you something, you have to *promise* promise. As in cross your heart. Because truthfully? If we're going to be friends, or even hang out, or even have any kind of talking-to-each-other thing going here, I need to be 100 percent convinced that I can trust you. Which is why you have to promise."

"I promise."

"Because, first of all, didn't you like wonder why I was hot-tailing it out of that stupid idiot football game that I never should have gone to to begin with but my mom kind of pushed me into it because I told her that I was kind of friendly with this one girl and I actually thought that maybe I'd have fun?"

"Huh?" I said. "What?"

"Did you not notice that I was trying to get out of there?"

"Of course I noticed. You were running away from me."

"You didn't help. And yeah, also, I totally did *not* want to deal with you. But there was this other thing too."

"The girls," I said. "Whoever they were. The ones who were talking about you behind your back so you could hear."

"No, I mean another other thing. The biggest thing of all."

"I'm medicated," I said. "You need to speak slowly and clearly." I tapped my head. "Me don't understand good."

She turned to me: she inhaled, she turned pink, she exhaled. "The thing is, I had a baby."

Words like a bomb, except not really, because a baby isn't a bomb, it's a baby.

"I *have* a baby," she corrected herself.

"A baby?"

"I think some of the skankier and meaner of these skanky mean bitches might have caught wind of it—I don't know. But they sure as hell weren't being real friendly toward me. I mean, at the game. I could have given them what-all, too, but they weren't worth it. Just be glad you're not a girl, is all I'm saying, because, yeah, dudes can be horrendous, obviously, war and all that, but girls can just be so insufferably *mean*."

Having once again had trouble following the zig-zag up-and-down of her conversational style, I opened my mouth, hoped I wasn't drooling, felt how heavy and unwieldy my tongue had suddenly become, and said, "You have a *baby*?"

"Yup."

"A real live baby? And not like, I don't know. A pretend one?" I myself couldn't remember the last time I had spoken with such intense idiocy.

"People have babies, you know."

"I guess."

"Please don't tell me that no one ever taught you about the birds and the bees."

"It's not that." Stammering. "More that—"

"Kind of hard to believe?"

"Kind of." How could Elizabeth, who couldn't have been more than five feet tall and a hundred pounds, have a baby? But because I obviously needed to prove my extreme insensitivity, I added, "Do you know who the father is?"

"*What?* Of course. He was my boyfriend. And we only did it twice. Just my luck."

"You knew him from school?"

"Something like that."

"Is the baby why you had to move?"

"*So* not your business."

"Is the baby, like—do you still have it?"

"Not *it*. Her. Angela. Angela's a her, and of course I still have her. What, you think I'd give up my own baby? God."

"Adoption?"

"You've seen too many movies."

"Look," I finally said. "I don't know about babies. How would I know about babies? I've never known a girl with a baby. I've never really known any babies at all. I'm just asking, is all. I know. I'm a moron."

"But not as moronic as a lot of people."

"If you say so."

"I did say so."

"That's what you said last night, too."

"No, I didn't."

"Yes, you did. You totally did. You 100 percent absolutely totally did."

Her face relaxed into something related to a smile, like the moment after you smile for the camera and then let yourself revert to what you really look like. "Keep your voice down," she said. "Like I really need to be even more wildly fashionably in-demand than I already am."

"On the other hand, hanging out with me is sure to boost your popularity ratings."

We both started laughing so hard that little bits of bread and puff-pastry spewed from our respective mouths like a tiny food volcano.

It was almost the end of first quarter.

10

When I wasn't sleeping or smoking, what I mainly did in the psyche ward was eat. The food wasn't very good but I ate it anyway, ate everything they had, with seconds on scrambled eggs and waffles and ice cream with every meal and ice cream bars too. Oh yeah: I also watched TV. I sat in the TV room with all the other underage psychos and manic-depressives and attempted-suicides and watched ancient reruns of *Seinfeld* and ancient reruns of *The Simpsons* and as much porn as we could, except we never really could because they kept those channels blocked. Plus there were girls in there: girls as young as I was; some younger. A girl named Jenny who had slit her wrists when she was twelve and then when that didn't work tried again, this time by swallowing a bottle of Ibuprofen except she threw most of it up. She was thirteen. A girl named Alison, aged fifteen, had what's called a "cutting disorder," which meant that she kept slivering

61

her own skin up, scarring herself, mainly with knives but sometimes with razor blades. Her thighs looked like an abstract impressionist painting, all bumpy red slashes, mottled purple splotches, worse even than my nicely dotted arms from all the places the tubes had punctured me, which by then were healing anyway, and were looking less and less like an ulcerous rash and more and more like old wood. And, of course, Susan: Susan the rubber-band snapper, except that she didn't snap rubber bands back then, not in the funny farm. She didn't have access to them, for one thing. None of us did. In fact, there was little in the way of material objects that we had access to, the theory being that almost anything could and would be used as weapons of self-destruction. In keeping with the theory of less-stuff-is-more-safe, the décor was similarly minimalist: the bed, the pillow, the nailed-to-the-wall TV sets, the nailed-to-the-floor tables, the hooks, not hangers, for your clothes, themselves screwed to the wall in such a way that you would need a forklift to unscrew them. We didn't even have real plates and cutlery but instead used the flimsiest throw-out kind.

Despite her starved look, Susan was the prettiest girl there. I could easily have stared at her all day except that the one or two times I worked up the courage to glance her way she gave me what I later learned to recognize as her you-are-so-ugly-and-gross-in-every-way-that-I-hope-you-die look. So despite her present contention that I stared at her, I didn't. I never had.

As for the others: Rufus had a spider tattooed onto his forehead. Alvin chain-smoked; his skin was a grayish white. Charlotte thought she was an egg. There we all were, the manic-depressives and the suicides and the chronic shoplifters and the bulimics, all of us together, watching TV. Then there was group therapy, and individual one-on-one therapy. Mainly what I did when I had private sessions was stare at the wine-red birthmark on my doctor's bald head. Every time I looked at it I saw something different: the face of an old man; a poodle; a pine tree; a pair of boots. The floor was speckled linoleum, and sometimes I could see faces in it too, though not as many as on my doctor's head. He asked me all kinds of questions and I answered them as best I could, but the thing is, there just wasn't all that much I could tell him. Like when he asked me about my family, and especially my parents: I didn't hate them. I didn't even dislike them. Truth was, I wasn't even all that *embarrassed* by them, at least not that much. They were my parents. I loved them. Mom drove me nuts, but I loved her. Dad: ditto. And Nate? He bugged me but even that wasn't any big deal. Like when he wanted to tag along, which was all the time, he got on my nerves. That, and he could be so annoying, jumping on me when I was just chilling, watching TV or whatever, and then, *wham*, there's Nate, flopping himself onto my lap. Or I'm walking down the sidewalk, and same thing, here comes little brother, and the next thing I know he's doing this kind of semi-hug semi-tackle thing. *Annoying*. My psychiatrist wanted to know about sex (which I couldn't tell him anything about other than the fact that one day I hoped to have it), my dreams (which were mainly nightmares), and whether I ever had sex dreams, which I did, and didn't want to talk about, and didn't remember much about anyway.

When he asked me about Sophie, all I did was cry.

I saw him every other day and had Group Therapy every morning. Group Therapy was all us youngsters sitting in a circle talking about our feelings, talking about how scared we were, just talking. There was this one kid who just kept saying that he hated his father and wanted to kill him. When anyone asked him why he wanted to kill him, he'd say: "Because if you ever met the dick you'd realize what a total dick-hole he is." Another kid spent every session picking at the same small scab on his arm. When it was my turn to talk about my parents, all I could say was that I loved them, and yeah, I fought with them, but they were my *parents*. . . . I loved them. Always had.

Most of the kids were quiet, but some of them weren't. Some of them were mean. Especially the girls. I'd never met girls like that before, with long fingernails and a way of looking at you that made you feel like a dried-up pile of crap with flies buzzing around it, and I was afraid of them. So yeah, I knew about how mean girls could be. On the other hand, I had always figured that being totally flat-out bonkers out-of-your-skull nuts is a pretty good excuse for less-than-pleasant behavior.

At night we were locked in with a couple of nurses stationed behind glass partitions to guard us. I slept in a room with Athens and this one other kid. His name was Litton and he barely talked at all except that once in a while, in the softest voice imaginable, so soft that it was more like the sound of a caterpillar crawling past than a whisper, he would say, "I want to go home." I wouldn't have even known that he'd tried to kill himself except that he had scars on both wrists, where he'd cut them with a razor blade. The one time I saw him get really upset was when I was discharged, and my parents picked me up. He sat on his bed and wouldn't even look at me. He wouldn't say good-bye. He wouldn't even meet my eyes, or rather, my eye. It was like he was three years old. It was just about the saddest thing I'd ever seen and I felt like roadkill, because even though he barely ever even talked, I was leaving him there like that.

Just before lights-out, the aides would come around with our meds—tranquillizers, sleeping pills. Five minutes later I would be so asleep it was as if I no longer existed at all.

My family came to visit me once a week, during Sunday family time, showing up at ten o'clock on the dot and staying the entire two hours that they were permitted to stay. We would sit across from one another in the lame so-called lounge and not talk about anything at all, while Mom chattered on and on, mainly about what Nate was up to, even though Nate would be sitting right there the whole time. She also talked about Buster. She told long, long stories about how Buster had lost his favorite bone, or about how there was a thunderstorm and Buster had hid under the bed for the entire time, shaking in terror, or about how he'd snuck into her vegetable garden and eaten all the strawberries.

"And I didn't even plant them this year," she would say. "I didn't really plant a garden at all. . . ." Then she'd let her voice trail off but it didn't matter because I could fill in her blanks: *How could I plant a garden when I was worried sick about you night and day that's all I could think about how did this happen what went wrong?* "The strawberries just came back by themselves. They're taking over!"

Dad would just jiggle his leg, like he does.

Nate would snort, check his cell phone, fiddle with it, and snort again.

After a while, I'd go back to my room to lie down, and Mom, following, would sit on the end of the bed while Dad and Nate leaned against the walls, jiggling their legs. Litton would be like "Hi." His mother and grandparents came to visit him, too: he didn't have a father. He had died when Litton was little.

Then my family would leave and I'd go watch TV.

Nothing happened there. Not during the day and not during the night, even though, one time, some kids were caught making out. I heard about it later. They made a big deal out of it, talking about how the rules were there for everyone's safety and comfort. But I thought those kids should have gotten a medal.

I don't know if it was the drugs I was on that made me sleep or if I was so tired from being in a reality of my own devising that I couldn't do anything else. I wasn't even bored. I was too tired to be bored. I was too out-of-it to be bored. I just didn't care. I would hug Athens to my chest and doze. I didn't even care about the hole in my face. All I cared about was Sophie.

One day at lunch after we'd gotten to know each other, I told Elizabeth all about it, including how Susan from the nuthouse had morphed into being Susan-at-TITSS, and how much she hated me, and how the only thing I could think about was Sophie. We'd forgone the cafeteria that day for a cement retaining wall on which someone had written, "Jessica and Pete 4-Ever" in bright-pink spray-painted scrawl, all loops and swirls. Under that someone else had written, "Mr. Watson is a master douche." I didn't think so, though. Strict, yes; chalk-throwing, most definitely. But master douche? Not really. It was chilly, sitting on the wall, but it was preferable to the cafeteria, where the combined smells of steamed vegetables and wet sponges and meatloaf and disinfecting floor cleaner reminded me of everything bad that had ever happened to me and ever could.

"I keep thinking that the reason they won't tell me about her is that I killed her. And Mom and Dad think that if I knew I'd jump off a bridge."

"Wait a minute," said Elizabeth. "First off, if you killed her, you'd be locked up. Trust me. And second off, I don't get it. Why don't you just go look for her? I mean, you must know where she lives, right?"

"Her home address, in Long Island, yes. And I've written to her there maybe a dozen times. All the letters come back stamped 'return to sender.'"

"Why don't you just go to her house, and knock on the door?"

"Are you crazy?"

"That would be you, remember?"

"Whatever. Elizabeth, think about it. How would I even manage to get there? I can't drive. I'm more or less under house arrest. I have no money. And if I were gone for more than an hour, my mother would break out in hives."

"Don't they have buses in Long Island?"

It was finally cold, the real deal, and I could see her words burst from her mouth as steam and then disappear into the gray air. The trees looked like they were shivering, up there against the sky, and the whole world smelled fresh and damp with brown-curling leaves. A watery stream dripped from my left nostril. Wiping my nose with the back of my hand, I said, "Say I do waltz on over to Sophie's house. Just toodle up there even though my parents would send the FBI out for me. I presume you'd help me on this errand?"

But instead of answering, she squinted at me and said, "Do you always do that?"

"What?"

"Forgo Kleenex?"

"You mean like this?" I said, taking another back-handed swipe, this time at the other, rightward nostril.

"Gross," she said, whipping out her cell phone, which I hadn't even heard buzz, and typing something into it with careful, quick thumbs.

As I waited for her to finish texting, it occurred to me that maybe Elizabeth had a point. How hard could it be to skip school and take the train into the city and then another to Long Island and then take a taxi or just walk or hitch a ride to Sophie's house? And if I could kind of like borrow Elizabeth's baby, and the three of us could kind of like pretend we were just a nice normal young couple, and that we're looking at houses to buy, except who would believe that, and what would the point be anyway? One look at us and it would be obvious we weren't looking at real estate; one look at us and it would be obvious we were too young to afford a broom closet in an abandoned building. And even if I managed to get out to Long Island and find the house, then what? *Knock knock, hi, I'm Josh? I know, you don't want to see me, but please, if you could just tell me where Sophie is, like, if she's okay?* Naturally, Sophie's parents would be overjoyed by my surprise visit, except they wouldn't be. What they'd be is alarmed. What they'd be is on the phone, calling the cops to come and have me arrested. Or at least that's what Mom, more or less, had hinted at, saying, "Obviously neither she nor her parents want to hear from you."

"So I assume you'd come with me on my errand of discovery?" I said.

"No can do," Elizabeth said, flatly. "Baby, remember? I can't just go off and leave her like that."

"Your mom can't watch her?"

"She takes care of her all day, while I'm in school. Then it's my turn. So Mom can work. She works nights."

"Want to hang out this afternoon?" I tried.

"What? Are you deaf? Didn't you hear me when I said that I have a baby at home? And a mother who works nights? My life is just a little more complicated than yours is, okay?"

"Nobody's life is more complicated than mine is," I said, but Elizabeth just rolled her eyes. The next minute, astoundingly, my cell phone beeped with the text-message sound. No one texted me except Mom and Dad, so it wasn't a big moment. Even so, it wasn't either of them. It was Fleur from TITSS. *Haven't seen you for a while. Hope you haven't forgotten us!*

11

A few days later, Mom found me in the attic.

"So this is where you go when you disappear," she said.

In my arms, Athens flopped like a rag. If you didn't know he was a stuffed animal, you would think he *was* a rag, brown and flaccid, the kind of thing you'd use to scrub floors. His neck was so scrawny that he looked like he'd met his death in a toy hangman's noose.

"Kind of."

"Oh, honey," she said. "I just wish you had friends. I mean, I get it: your old friends are all in college, and the kids in school are younger than you. But your classmates are only one year younger—which isn't such a big difference." I didn't reply.

"Isn't there anyone you like at your meetings?"

Settling in against the suitcase where I'd stashed my emergency cigs, Mom sat beside me and gave Athens a little pat between the ears. Together, we watched the dust motes swirl in the warm late afternoon sunshine.

"Anyone at all?" she said.

"Not really," I said, thinking of Susan with her hissing noises and sharp white teeth.

"What about that girl at school?"

"What girl at school?"

"The girl you hang out with at school? The one with the scar?"

"*What?*" I said. "How do you know about her?"

"Don't be like that, Josh. I'm glad you have a friend. I just wish I could meet her, is all. Why don't you bring her around here some time?"

"How do you even know about her?"

"I'm not spying on you, if that's what you think. Your brother told me."

"What?" My voice was rising in my throat now. "What did *Nate* tell you? What does *Nate* have to do with anything? Why is this his business?"

"Oh, come on, honey. I asked him, after the football game, you know, did you have any friends, anyone to eat lunch with. Because believe it or not I was in high school once, and I still remember that terrifying, excruciating feeling of not having anyone to eat with in the cafeteria. That's all."

"Mom! I can't believe you're poking into my life like that! I'm eighteen!"

"Sweetheart, listen, I really don't want to upset you, but I want to ask you about your new friend. Nate said no one really knows anything about her. Are you sure she's—is she good company for you?"

"I thought you just said you were happy that I have a friend."

"And I am, honey. Truly. I just want to make sure that the people you spend time with are healthy, you know, good for you."

Just then, that very second, I got another miraculous text message, and for a moment, I got excited. Given that Mom was right next to me, it wasn't her, which left three possibilities: Fleur, Elizabeth, or Dad.

I tapped on it. It was a message from Susan: *Loser.*

Even though it was from someone who I already knew hated me, as I took the word on the screen into my brain, I felt a jolt of brand-new misery spread into my guts and bones. Then, just as suddenly, I got angry.

What was her problem? What did I ever do to her to make her hate me so much? Like she was such a winner? Sure, she was pretty—extremely pretty—but since when did that give you an excuse to dump all over everyone else?

"Honey? I think at the very least it's not too much to ask that you bring this new friend of yours home, so Dad and I can meet her." She leaned forward. "Wait a sec, something's jabbing me in my back."

Twisting around to find out what was sticking her in the back, she found my secret nicotine stash. I braced for the ensuing lecture.

"Oh, Josh. Oh, honey. I hate that you smoke, but I have to tell you that you simply can't ever smoke up here, not even once. The whole house could go up in flames. Can you promise me?"

"Can I promise you what? That I won't set the house on fire? Or that I'll bring my friends by so you can check them out? Or that I'll promise to be a good boy and go to all the school football games? Or that I'll go to all my TITSS meetings and be friends with all the other good boys and girls there?"

She didn't get the humor. Probably because it wasn't funny. "Is that what you want me to promise, Mom?"

"No."

"You just want me to promise that I won't ever trouble you again, is that it?"

"No, but I would like a promise from you to never smoke up here, or in the house, at all."

"I'm eighteen, Mom. I can smoke if I want to."

"There are a lot of things you can do if you want to. I'm talking about things I'd like you to do, for me—for all of us."

"Dear God."

"Honey? Please? Bring your new friend by some day. So Dad and I can meet her."

"You mean so Dad and you can grill her."

"We just really really need to know who your friends are, honey. After all, with—oh, never mind."

"With who? With what? What were you going to say?" But I knew what she was going to say: she was going to say something about Sophie. Then a thought struck me: what if she decided to go looking for additional contraband and found the photo of Sophie I'd hidden? Then what?

"Nothing. Just that we'd like to get to know your new friend."

Another text message from Susan: *Lard butt.*

It arrived as Mom was saying, "I've been meaning to ask you, Josh—do those boys at school still harass you?"

"Did you go and make some stupid report on them?"

"Honey, I'm your *mother*—it's my job to protect you, remember?"

Which was when the rage got the better of me, welling up like a wall of blood, like a building crashing on me, like a tidal wave, or a volcano, or my own veins collapsing inward, blocking everything out and then . . .

By tomorrow she would find my one and only photo of Sophie and dispose of it. As the thought landed, I could feel the anger inside me grow and spread, like one of those pebble-sized sponges that you put in water, and voilà, a few minutes later, it's taken on the size and shape of a salmon. It's all I can do to get up off my backside and down the steep stairs, me and Athens together, come on, Athens, just you and me, buddy, only Mom's following me down the stairs saying—*Blah blah where are you going Josh what's wrong Josh what happened blah Josh yap yap blah Josh* —only I'm not listening, because what I want to do is, I want to punch her, I want to push her down the stairs, she doesn't understand *anything*, and I'm truly and very sorry that I've messed up her perfect life, messed up everyone's, that I've already cost them more money than I'll probably ever make in my entire lifetime, and that I'm ugly and fat and embarrassing, and maybe if I fell down the stairs or ran into traffic or: boom. Gone. Why not? I don't even remember the first time I almost died. How hard could it be to do it for real? Why won't they tell me what happened? Why won't they tell me how I ended up in that hospital, how I almost lost my eye? Did a bong explode in my face? Did I get into a knife fight? Was I mugged? Did I do it myself, to myself, by myself? They all say the same thing, that they don't know about it, that all they know is that someone called 911 and the next thing you know, I'm being carted away, unconscious and bleeding, the EMS people pumping emergency blood into me so I won't bleed to death, my eyeball smashed in. Only they won't tell me what happened, no one will, not Dr. Chang in the hospital, not Dr. Rose, not Mom or Dad or Nate. Maybe Athens will tell me what happened—*What happened, Athens?*—but of course he just looks at me with his black button eyes and doesn't answer, *Of course he doesn't, he's a stuffed dog, stupid, he's made of cloth, and you're too old to be sleeping with him anyhow, if Susan finds out about you and Athens you'll be an even bigger disaster, an even bigger laughing stock, except, shit, you already told her, you told everyone at TITSS about him. First time around, they locked you up with a bunch of unsuccessful, loser, amateur suicides . . . and now your only friend is a single teen mother with a scar like a stripe of melted red plastic.*

I've got to get out of here. You understand, don't you, Athens? You and me . . . as I run down the steps the cats look at me with their stupid eyes and Buster starts to bark, *Take me on a walk! Take me on a walk!* But it's too late, because I'm out the door and pounding down the stairs and out the driveway and now I'm on the sidewalk, and I'm running past the Jensens' house where I used to go when I was little to pee in the bushes, past Mrs. Rudd, who has been in a wheelchair since before I was born and who no one sees, past the Letners, who have like a dozen cats, and the Scoppetuols, who have barbecues all summer long, the smell of cooking hamburgers and steaks wafting over four, five houses to ours and making me hungry, and then I'm at the end of the block and I'm still running, my heart pounding, my feet flapping and slapping on the pavement, until I'm in the park—the park where I used to run off-season, just to stay in shape—and I'm really huffing and puffing, and I can feel my blubber blubbering up and down, but I keep going anyway. I want my heart to burst. I want my brain to explode. My lungs are pure garbage. I've got to stop.

But I don't, not right away. Instead, it's not until I'm at the far end of the park that I run out of gas completely and stop. I'm stooped over myself, trying to breathe, when a bunch of little kids come over and just kind of stand there, looking at me. I look up. "What?"

"You okay, mister?" one of them, a little boy, says.

"Why shouldn't I be?"

"You look kind of like you're going to get sick."

"Well, I'm not. I'm fine."

"Plus you got that eye patch."

"I'm aware."

Kid just looks at me, all wide-eyed and oblivious and obvious and innocent. "What's your dog's name?"

"What dog?"

"Dang. That dog you got in your hand."

I look at my hand. I'm clutching Athens by his right ear.

"Athens," I say.

"Athens? What kind of name is Athens?"

"Why? You got a better one?"

He tilts his head sideways, like Buster does when he wants a treat, and then, brightening, says, "If he were mine? I'd name him *Mister Twister.*"

"What are you saying? You saying that I should give him to you?"

"No, Mister. You keep him. I got plenty of my own stuff. I just like my name better."

And with that, he skips off to join his friends, and I straighten up. It's then that I see the cross-country team jogging by, on the other side of a baseball diamond. Nate's out in front, his chest heaving and his legs like scissors, slicing the air.

12

After that, I started working out. I would plop along, in my running shoes and sweats, and by the time I was done, I felt like an old man on the brink of a heart attack. I'd go to the park and back; the lake and back. Then I started running around the park. Or I'd do a loop: the park, the lake, home. I can't say I enjoyed it, or even found it mildly satisfying. But after a while I didn't feel quite so dead inside, and I lost weight, too, something I wasn't even aware of until, one day, Elizabeth squeezed my upper arm and told me she could feel an actual muscle in there. Only she put it even more bluntly: "Hey, something is growing under your flab."

"Thanks."

"Any time."

It turned out that the misery of running was better than the misery of being half-awake and half-asleep. It was better than endlessly debating the chorus of voices in my head. It was even better than thinking of all the ways I would make the insects suffer once I decided to finally pummel them to a group pulp, even though, these days, they mainly stayed away.

On the minus side, my new routine made cigarettes less appealing, and I missed the cool-hot jolt of soothing, smooth nicotine filling my blood and brain. On the plus side, it gave me an excuse to stay away from TITSS, where I would be sure to see Susan, who had continued to send me all kinds of nasty text messages that stayed in my mind long after I had blocked her.

Dr. Rose didn't buy it, though. "You're getting stronger, Josh," he said. "You can handle this." So I decided that I'd confront Susan and tell her what a complete bitch-job she was, and why I wasn't going to put up with it. It gave me pleasure, a small shrill thrill, to imagine it: how my words would flay her alive, force her into begging me for mercy and forgiveness. Which I knew was utter crap, as big a bunch of crap as her own crap, but which I kept thinking about anyway, a little private movie that played over and over again in my mind, always with the same pleasing ending:

"Oh God, Josh, I'm just so sorry—and by the way, you look fabulous. Have you lost weight?"

"It's okay. And yes, I've been running."

"Dude. You look *hot*."

"Yeah, right."

"No, I mean it. Want to come over to my house later? My parents are away until next week."

It didn't exactly go down that way. Susan was too busy snapping at the rubber bands on her wrist to notice anything, including me. Meantime, Fleur was giving a truly scintillating talk on the subject of drugs that I had heard a thousand times before and everyone else in the room had too.

Not about Haldol, Prolixin, Navane, Loxapine, Stelazine, Trilafon, Mellaril, Ritalin, Methylin, Metadate, Concerta, Wellbutrin, Tenex, Clonindine, etcetera, but about *drug* drugs, the kind you take for fun.

The bottom line, she pointed out, was: you can't. Not if you were like us. Not ever again. Not even a single puff, of a single joint, on a single lonely night, and that's because, she said, as if we all didn't already know it, any slight burp or ripple in our neurotransmitters could send us dancing back off into the stars, never to find our way back to the mother ship.

Susan snapped her rubber band so hard even I could feel it, while across the way, a kid I had never seen before looked like he was going to lose his lunch.

"Typically, the urge to self-medicate, to use marijuana, or alcohol, as a way to take the edge off, is strong. But it's poison. And that's what we're here for, all of us, and not just me: so you can reach out, over the phone if you can't get to a meeting, and talk things through."

Snap.

"If you can catch yourself, become aware of that awful feeling *before* you reach for your drug of choice, you'll have a lot better chance of learning to tolerate your own internal weather."

Snap, snap, snap, snap, snap.

"That's it for today," she finally said. "Who would like to start?"

For the longest while, no one said anything. Then Susan, as was her habit, broke the ice. "It came back," she said, looking across the table directly at me.

The thing is, at Western High, it was so easy to get your hands on weed that there was an entire page on Urban Dictionary devoted to the school's weed-centric reputation. There was no corner of the school that was free of the rich and pungent smell of freshly smoked smoke, of kids getting high on the little rise of brambly woods just on the other side of the school grounds.

I got my own first stash from an upperclassman on the cross-country team. We used to get high after practice and then just laugh and laugh. And then I started to get high and cry. Then I'd get high and everyone, including me, looked like a creature from outer space, and then I started hearing voices. I don't remember when I personally became disconnected with normative reality, but that other part—how the voices became Voices, which told me that I had been chosen for great things—that part I do remember.

What happened was that I was smoking hash out of a bong with a friend and we were laughing our heads off and then I went home and looked in the mirror and saw green gook coming out of my eyes and green smoke coming out of my ears and I freaked out, scared out of my mind, until, voilà, this angel came up to me, personally, to have a chat. I knew it was an angel because he had the whole angel look down pat: the long white robe belted by a cord, probably made out of donkey hair or something but I didn't look closely enough to do a good study of it; the long if trimmed beard; the long, hippie hair; the sandals; the halo around his head, and, of course, the giant white feathery wings. And he was like: *Yo, Josh, dude! Don't stress, man. You're safe. You're safe in My arms. I will always be with you. I will always protect you. I will always love you.*

And I was like: *Huh? Who are you?*

And he was like: *Don't mess with Me, man. You know exactly who I am.*

Then I was all: *Oh, yippee!*

Then he was all: *You have been chosen.*

And I was all: *Who, me?*

Know that we are all angels of the one true truth.

I was so messed up that I even thought about going to get Mom and Dad but was too scared. Instead, I took a really long cold shower. By the time I had toweled off, the weed was wearing off. I was tired. I cried into Buster's fur and then climbed into bed, where I cried into Athens's fur and finally, with Buster drooling on the pillow next to me, fell asleep.

13

The very first thing in the hazy gray dawn of pre–first period when kids are more zombie than human, more hoodie than eyes, Coach Dupe, my old cross-country coach, nabbed me, laid a coach-heavy hand on my shoulder, and said, "I had a talk with your mother, Josh."

"Huh?"

"She told me you've started running again."

"If you can call it running."

"Why don't you think about joining the team?"

When I didn't say anything, he said, "You'd be an inspiration for the other boys."

I was so surprised that it took me a while to formulate a response. Finally, though, it came out, in all its raw glory. "An inspiration? Just take a look at me. Do I look like a runner to you?"

"I'm not talking about what you look like, son. What I'm saying is, you've still got heart. Think about it from a freshman's point of view. Think about what an example you'd set, of courage, of guts. And to tell the truth, I want you on the team because, from what I've seen, you've still got it. And it wouldn't hurt to drop the extra weight. You'd feel better. It's not your fault, what happened to you, you know? Everyone knows that. The kids here—even the biggest nitwits—are on your side. Staff too. Everyone is. You shouldn't feel so self-conscious."

Coach Dupe was one of those guys who, if he weren't wearing a baseball cap with a whistle around his neck, you'd think something was wrong with him. He had thick gray hair and jowls that tended to take on a life of their own. He was studying me so intently with his gray-green eyes that I blushed.

"What about Nate?" I finally said. "He'd freak."

"Why would he freak? He's your brother."

Because ever since I'd come back home last June he'd been doing his best to avoid me? Because I embarrassed him? Because why should he be dragged down by having his bigger and fatter and uglier and weirder big brother hanging around?

"The last thing he'd want is me tagging along with his cross-country bros," I said. "It's not his fault that he's normal."

"Oh, come on."

"It's just that I don't want to mess up his party. He's really into it."

And with that, Coach Dupe brightened a bit and, leaning into the scuffed-up barf-orange of the locker fronts, said, "Your brother has it, all right. He's not quite up to where you once were. But he's something else. And what about that time he ran yesterday, at the county meet? Amazing."

I didn't even know that there was a meet yesterday, let alone the county meet, which was always the big deal, the one we all went crazy over, psyching ourselves up for it, each of us determined to run until our guts spilled out.

"He didn't tell me about it," I said.

"Well, he should have. Kid did a 5k in well under seventeen, not only broke his own record but every school record except yours. He was a second under your best time."

"Sixteen minutes, eighty-nine seconds," I said automatically, remembering the numbers flashing up as I crossed the finish line with everyone around me cheering and yelling my name and Mom screaming "Go! Go! Go!" and Dad just behind her, grinning, and all the kids patting me on the back, my heart pounding so fast I could barely hear anything, the sweat pouring off my forehead. I was walking slowly, trying not to vomit, trying to still the spinning world when I heard it: "First Place goes to Josh Cushing and Western High."

You forced yourself to keep going, through all the exhilarating pain. That's what I loved most about it.

"Your brother blew them away," said Coach Dupe. "You may want to congratulate him."

This is incredibly embarrassing to say out loud, but before I went off my rocker, I could do no wrong. I'm pretty sure that my looks, pre-insanity, didn't hurt, being tall and thin and athletic, with girls always flirting with me, except that because I am/was on the shy side, I didn't really like any of them back—except of course Sophie, who I loved. Mom would tease and say that having me for a son was like finally having a cool high school boyfriend, which was all one big joke, because obviously Mom was married to Dad and they still canoodled and mainly Mom just beamed Mom-beams on me all the time: Josh, her pride and joy; Josh, who had a special destiny, and would therefore one day reach the heights of. . . of what?

It didn't matter that I never ran for class office, or played the piano or got great grades or really *anything*, other than running, that put me above the fray. I was special. She never said so, not in so many words, but even when I was little I knew that that's how she secretly felt. *Every-one* knew it. She tried hard not to show it, but it was so obvious that me and Nate and Dad would joke about it, saying things like how, when she was in a bad mood, I was the only one who could make her laugh, or how she should ask me to take her to the prom. It didn't matter how busy she was at work: when I was little, she would plan my birthday parties for weeks; later, she read all my papers; went to all my meets. She fussed over Nate too, but it was different, slightly more muted, and when we pointed that out to her, she'd say, "It's birth order. Of course I love you boys equally."

But not, I thought, anymore. Not now that I had become person-to-be-managed-at-all-costs. As I made my way home after school, thinking about how Mom had gone to Coach Dupe, my voices wouldn't stop needling me: *Mommy always shows up! She always shows up! She always shows up to get me!* And it didn't help when, not three seconds after I'd closed the front door behind me, she came trotting downstairs, with this big dumb fake smile on her face, and said, "I need to discuss something with you."

"Yeah, well I need to discuss something with you, too."

"Go ahead," she said.

"Why do you have to go sticking your nose into every corner of my business?"

"Excuse me?"

"Coach Dupe, Mom. He's trying to get me to join the team."

"Really? I think that's a wonderful idea."

"Yeah, because it's yours. Because you called him and told him to go and have a little chat with me."

"For your information," she said, "I did call him, but it wasn't about you, it was about your brother. Apparently your brother is such a good runner that he's being recruited by various colleges, and I wanted to talk to Coach Dupe about it. So what if I mentioned that you'd started running too?"

The funny thing is that though her explanation made sense, it didn't calm me down at all. Nor did it calm down the incessant, irritating, annoying inner voices, who were now saying, *Liar liar pants on fire!*

Mommy's looking out for her sweet little cupcake woo-woo little dumpling darling poo poo pants.

". . . and sweetheart, I'm delighted that you're running again. Your dad is too."

Tell her to shove it . . . Tell her to stick a needle in her eye, to swallow poison and then die . . .

"Have you told Dr. Rose?"

"Whatever," I said, defeated, with shame welling up in me, shame that had no bottom and no source, because the more I thought about it, the more I didn't know where it came from.

Then Mom said, "But anyway, Josh, Coach Dupe aside, there is something I need to talk to you about."

"Of course there is."

"Just put the sarcasm on hold for a minute, if you please. This is serious."

"What do you know?"

"This Elizabeth person, who you hang out with."

"Elizabeth," I said. "Her name is Elizabeth. Not *this Elizabeth person.*"

"Elizabeth Rinaldi."

"How do you know her last name?"

"Honey," she said, sounding wounded.

"I mean it, Mom! What does Elizabeth have to do with anything?"

"I know this is hard for you to understand," Mom began. "But Dad and I, we have to—as your parents, part of our jobs is to help you navigate back into regular, mainstream life."

"I'm not an infant!"

"I'm aware," Mom said. "But you're still pretty heavily medicated, Josh. And your judgment may still be slightly impaired. It's not your fault. I'm not saying anything like that. Just that Dad and I have an interest in helping you regain your health, in every way."

"Do you *want* me to hang myself from the rafters?"

"Don't even joke about that, Josh. Good God. Do you think you're the only one who's suffered here?"

I plopped myself and my backpack down on the sofa, and as Mom talked on, I felt worse and worse, angrier and angrier, more and more hollowed-out, and more and more ashamed and panicked and *bad*— like my insides, my innards, my very soul was made of garbage, filth, corruption, a combination of vomit, dog poop, people poop, dead rodents, dead worms, and shards of glass. In a manner of speaking. If you know what I mean.

"Listen, honey, I know this is hard, I really do. I mean, I really really do. But trust me, I have to know what's going on in your life. It's not really that different from when you were younger and I always made sure, when you were going to a party, that the parents were home. Remember? I'm not saying that you don't have a right to your own life, because of course you do."

And me, I was thinking about this time when I was twelve and I went back behind the garage at my friend Tim's (now at Rutgers) and with my other friend Joe (GW) and a pile of dirty magazines that one of them had fished out of someone's uncle's closet, and how we stared and stared and made stupid jokes to cover up our combination of sheer outright amazement and sheer outright horniness. And then Tim stashed his porn in an unused trash can back behind some bramble bushes in the very back corner of the yard, and we went inside to the kitchen and ate two boxes of Pop-Tarts.

". . . but the bottom line is that your friend has a kind of shaky story. I mean, I'm not stupid, honey, and I'm a trained lawyer. I spent my entire career working with juveniles who for one reason or another got themselves into a world of trouble, so if there's one thing I know about, it's risk-taking behavior, and what a slippery-slope it can be, almost like a drug, or an addiction."

"Elizabeth doesn't use drugs," I said. "She's the most non-drug person I've ever met."

"Well, I've been doing a little research, and there's reason for me to think that your friend might be troubled."

"Jesus, Mom."

"Look, honey. I'm not accusing her, or you, of anything. I'm just being—well, extra careful, is all. Call me a hover-mother, fine. But it's my right, after all we've been through, all of us, as a family."

"Oh God. I hate it when you talk that way."

She leaned forward. "All I'm saying is—look, just invite her over, okay? For dinner. For whatever. I just want to meet her, is all. To talk with her. Is that too much to ask?"

"Actually," I said, "yes. Yes it is."

And then I saw myself, in my mind's eye: Me: lying crumpled in a corner wearing soiled sweat clothes. Me: clutching Athens. Me: coming out of a bathroom stall, looking like I just shot up. Me: blood streaming out of my left eye socket. Me: whimpering, whimpering. Me: with something in my hand, something sharp, something gleaming.

She must succumb. It is part of the plan.

". . . you may not want to help yourself, and God knows that Nate's been unhelpful—but Dad and I can't just stand here and allow you to get involved with someone who may or may not be trustworthy."

But I was gone—gone gone, my mind whirling, my fists clenched, my breathing like flecks of metal in my lungs. Then I was on my feet. Then I was down the stairs and out the door and into the cold late afternoon of the year's dreariest month.

Two or three blocks later, it started to snow, and as a flake landed on my tongue, I remembered the last time I'd run in the snow—a year ago? Less? More? I couldn't remember: all I remembered was the run itself, the exact pounding of it, the exact darkness swirling into my head. There was a winter storm, and the trains weren't running, but I had to see Sophie—so I decided to run into the city.

It was only six miles to the George Washington Bridge, nothing for me, not in the shape I was in. From there I could take a subway. She'd have to talk to me. I just had to see her. I had to see her to tell her that I loved her. I had to tell her that one day we'd be married, me and her, that we were destined to be together.

I loved her so much.

I started down Mystic Street, turned the corner onto Bellevue, then Church Street, then Linden Avenue, then on and on, I didn't even have to look at any map or any street signs, my feet knew where to go, and the air was chilled and damp and cold, the snow falling in time to my heart beat, my blood pumping perfectly, perfectly into my temples, into my synapses, into my feet, and I felt like I was flying, it was almost like one of those flying dreams, except I was awake, and I was running, running toward Sophie.

There were almost no cars on the streets. Just parked cars, and lit-up houses, lit-up windows, lit-up Christmas displays. It was just me and the falling snow and the black branches and the parked cars.

As I approached the GW Bridge from above, I saw the river lying low and elegantly, all gray and shimmering, a long satin ribbon, a perfect pool of still gray quietude, and the red taillights of cars going east and the white headlights of cars coming west, and then there was the city itself, rearing up, and the bridge, with its swooping sails of steel ropes.

I was down on the bridge itself then, running past the cars the trucks the taxis the vans the bleating beeping red and white lights disappearing in the snow, I could fly right off the bridge but I knew I couldn't. I was running I wasn't a bird I was a boy but I had wings on my feet—

And right there I saw it: The Face of God. Only He didn't have a face, not a human face, anyway. He didn't have eyes, or a nose, or a mouth, or a chin or hair or ears. But I knew that the shimmering light I saw before me was God. I just knew it. And I stopped.

"You are my Beloved."

But he said no more, and as I stood there, the snow blowing in my face, I knew He wanted to tell me something else, but that He was waiting for me, that I had to ask Him.

"WHAT?"

The wind blew.

"WHAT IS IT YOU WANT ME TO DO?"

The traffic blundered by, a roar and a whoosh and a grimy growl.

"Fly, my darling," the voice said. "Fly over the water."

Ah—the river and the bridge and the city. The perfection of it all. The bliss. I took a step forward. And I saw that the bridge was an illusion, and the air around it was an illusion, and I myself was an illusion, as all of us were part of the great cosmos, the great mind of the universe.

"SPREAD YOUR WINGS AND FLY."

I took another step forward.

Then I heard, "Kid? Kid? Hey! WHAT ARE YOU DOING?"

I was looking out at the river.

"ARE YOU ALL RIGHT?"

And then there was honking and someone had his hands on me and then someone else did too.

"He won't talk."

"Is he a jumper, do you think?"

"I don't know, but he won't talk."

"Better call the cops."

But I didn't want the cops. I didn't want anything but to find Sophie.

"Son?"

I turn around. Two or three grown-ups were standing just below me.

"Come on down, son. Here, let me help you."

And as I came down there was an arm around my shoulder, a man's arm, and he was saying, "You okay, kid? You gave me a scare."

"I'm okay," I said. "I'm—I'm a runner."

"You sure you're a runner and not a jumper?"

"I'm going to—" But then I wasn't anymore. I was going to fly over the water to find Sophie, and make the world whole again, and because I was an angel, and I could fly, I would fly her with me to the garden of innocence and beauty. But then I saw how dumb that was. I was just a kid. I couldn't fly.

But I could run. I headed back to where I'd come from and it was only when I was completely lost in Bergen County that I got my cell phone out of my back pocket. Twenty minutes later, Nate pulled up in Mom's Toyota, speakers blaring, saying, "Get in, jerk-face. You ruined my afternoon. Again. Mom's been so completely freaked out that Dad made her take some drug to calm her down. And Dad—he's not too happy either. Why do you have to be such a dick-head?"

And the next thing I remembered was that I was back home, with my mother, in great gulping tears, her arms around my neck, and my father behind her, his arms around the both of us.

14

This time, when I got back from my non-run in the non-snow, Mom was worried, but not freaked out, whereas Dad, who had gotten home in the interim, was merely annoyed. I bolted up the stairs to the attic, where I unearthed my precious Sophie photo, restashing it inside one of my cross-country trophies in my room. I had to unscrew the gold-colored champion-running guy from the top of the champion-running cup thing, which was a depressing reminder of how far I myself had fallen from the running whiz I had once been, but at least this way I knew where my one Sophie was, hidden and safe and close. While I was at it, I rehid my emergency cigarettes. I'm telling you, I was on a roll.

Next, I called Elizabeth, who didn't pick up, so I left a message, the first I had left, anywhere, since . . . I'm going to say before I lost my eye.

"Please call me. I remembered something." But she didn't. So I called again. No dice. So I texted her. Nothing. I texted her a few dozen more times. *I need to talk to you.* Still nothing. Was she hurt? Had her baby had some kind of baby fever and had to be taken to the hospital? *Please please call me Elizabeth call me please.* Nothing. Not at one in the morning. Not at two in the morning. Not at three. By morning I looked and felt like something that had been run over, and things only got worse, when, at school, Elizabeth wouldn't even look at me. In the halls, in the cafeteria, on the sidewalks where geeks mingle with nerds who mingle with punks who mingle with jocks, it's yesteryear all over again, with her scurrying away from me as fast as her little legs will carry her.

Text from me: *What. Did. I. Do?*

Text from her:

Text from me: *What. The. Hell.*

Text from her:

Text from me: *I really need to talk to you.*

Text from her:

It was Athens who suggested that if I really needed to talk to Elizabeth so badly, I should go to her house, where she was sure to be, at least according to what she had told me about how she had to go home right away after school to be with her baby so her mother could go to work. The only problem was that I had no idea where she lived.

"Look it up, stupid," Athens said in his silent stuffed-dog whisper-voice. "How many people can there be whose last name is Rinaldi?"

"In New Jersey? Are you kidding?"

"Don't be lazy," said Athens.

Boom: there it was, in WhitePages.com. With an address on Bay Street. Number 21. The other end of town, and me barred from driving.

"So run there," Athens whisper-murmured.

I didn't know if I could, though, not without busting a lung or perhaps collapsing from a ruptured heart and dying on the street. Mom would have a field day. And it was already four o'clock; there were only about two hours of daylight left.

"Mom will freak," I said.

"Not if you get back before she gets home," Athens averred. "Or you could just, you know, leave a note telling her that you're out on a run and not to worry." He looked at me like *Duh*.

Number 21 Bay Street was a red-brick triple-decker not unlike the other buildings on the street, with three doorbells, all of them unmarked. I rang all three.

"Who are you?" a man's voice said through the speaker a moment later, and when I explained, he said, "Top floor."

I rang the top button again, and waited.

Finally, Elizabeth herself appeared, in person, in the foyer. "Go away," she said, just loud enough for me to hear her through the window at the top of the door.

"But Elizabeth!" I yelled. "I ran here—it must be four miles—to see you. I don't understand! Why won't you talk to me?"

"Curious, were you?" she yelled back.

"What?"

"Wanted to see for yourself what my pathetic and sad existence looks like?"

"What? No—no, I swear, Elizabeth, no. No, of course not."

"And I suppose your mother sent you over here to spy on me?"

"What?"

"Your mother."

"What about her?"

"Oh God. *Really?*"

"Huh?"

"Then what are you doing here?"

"I wanted to see you."

"*What?*"

"You're like—you're my best friend."

"Not anymore!"

With that, I started crying. It was truly pathetic, how easily I broke down, how readily the water works flowed, how girl-like and babyish and soft and ultrasensitive I was. I read an article this one time about a woman who became a man—in other words, he was transgender—and he said that now that he was male, he didn't cry any more. I was the opposite. I was sopping my own shirt with my tears.

"I give up," Elizabeth said, finally letting me in, where I followed her up the stairs and into her apartment, where the first thing I noticed was the baby. She was this tiny little thing, dressed in white footie-pajamas, lying on her back in a playpen in the middle of the living room, making baby noises, and she was so beautiful she turned the entire room into a sliver of warm light. I stood over the playpen, staring, until at last Elizabeth tapped me on the shoulder.

"Explain," she said. "Why are you here?"

"I remembered this thing—I thought I could fly. I had to tell you. It was—I was on the GW Bridge and I thought I could fly. And also, my mother—"

"Don't tell me about your mother! Your mother is trying to ruin my life!"

"You've got it all wrong," I said. "Mom's job is to ruin my life, not yours."

"She's like, *investigating* me."

"What?"

"You really didn't know?"

"What? No! What? What do you mean?"

She must have believed me when I said I didn't know, because her whole body relaxed as she explained that a social worker had visited, out of the blue, asking questions.

"What are you saying, Elizabeth? My mother sent a social worker over here? Why? And anyway, that doesn't even make sense. How could my mother send a social worker to your house? How would she even know where you live? How would she even know your last name?"

"I'm not sure," Elizabeth said. "All I know was that that social worker was poking around and around, and it was weird."

"But why on earth—I mean, so what? Even if a social worker did want to know stuff, so what? It isn't illegal to have a baby, is it?"

"She pretended that it was about Angela," Elizabeth said. "Making all these cooing, what-a-sweet-little-girl noises, but what she really wanted to know was other stuff."

"What other stuff?"

And out it came: "The thing is, I have a record."

Just like that. Like: the thing is, I have a headache. Or: the thing is, I hate sushi. Or: the thing is, I'm tired. Only it was about having a record.

"A record." I myself was turning into a record.

"It was JV, but still," she said.

"JV," I said.

"I mean, it didn't add up to much, considering."

"What'd you do?" I finally said.

"Don't look at me like that, dude! I didn't kill anyone! All I did was some minor shoplifting. Okay, maybe it was more than minor. It was stupid, I know—really stupid. But I'd just found out I was pregnant and it was already too late to have an abortion—long story but let's just put it out there that I didn't know I was pregnant until like four months before Angela was born—and the next thing I know I'm in the mall trying to stuff all these baby things into my bag: little booties, little hats, teensy T-shirts, all kinds of shit."

"You went to court for stealing baby booties?"

"More than booties. I mean, a lot more. I just kept not getting caught until one day I was. I actually managed to steal a stroller, a whole stroller, I just strolled it right out of the store and kept going until I was back at my house. And a bunch of other stuff, too. Which was particularly ridiculous given that Mom was totally supportive. Not that she wanted me to be an unwed underage mom. But she wasn't all mean about it. She was more like 'we'll figure it out one day at a time.'"

"You stole a stroller? How'd you get away with it?"

"As I said, I strolled." She flopped on the sofa, her arms trailing after her.

"But if that's all you did—I mean, stealing is bad, against the law, everyone knows that. But a little larceny isn't the end of the world, is it?"

"It's complicated."

"Couldn't be any more complicated than my own recent history."

She waved my trenchant and amusing remark away, saying, "I don't need anyone, your mother, your father, your lawyer or psychiatrist, not to mention teachers, or anyone at all at school, to know a thing about it. We moved here so I could start again, fresh, to put all the mess from back home behind me—Mom's idea—and it sucks in every way possible but will suck even more if suddenly it turns out that every kid in school knows about what happened."

"You mean that you got pregnant and had a baby?" I mumbled idiotically.

"And second," she said, ignoring me, "if some social worker goes around sniffing and digging and asking questions, it could get out all over again, and Barry could come looking for me, and honestly I don't even want to think about it."

"Barry?" I finally said. "He was your boyfriend?"

"That's one way to put it."

"But I thought you told me—"

"I did."

"So what's the big deal? I mean—if Barry was your boyfriend, and mistakes happen—and I admit, an actual baby isn't something you just shrug off, but still . . ."

I was basing my thinking on myself and my own (former) friends, who were as afraid of making a baby as they were desperate to have sex. I myself never had the worry, of course, as it's hard to get a girl pregnant if you've never done it.

"It wasn't so straight-forward, okay?"

"Oh, I get it," I said, finally getting it. "It was a hook-up. So what? Kids do that."

Which is when Elizabeth, who was always so tough, turned the tables on me, and, bursting into tears, said, "It wasn't a hookup."

"So?"

"Barry was my teacher." Then, when I didn't respond other than to stare at her, she added, "American history."

Then, all of a sudden, I saw things clearly. "You were raped?"

"What?"

"Did Barry rape you? You can tell me."

At that very moment, and as if my question had made her remember her two-celled beginning, Angela started to cry. Elizabeth went over to the playpen, picked her up, and started to sing. When Angela calmed down again, I said, "I'm serious, Elizabeth. You can tell me anything."

"That's cool, dude," she said. "But I wasn't raped."

Then there was like—this moment. This moment of awe. Seeing that baby in Elizabeth's arms like that, I understood, for the first time, that Elizabeth wasn't acting out a role or making up a story or being dramatic: she really was a mother. She was a mother, and Angela was her baby.

"Can I hold her?" I said.

She handed the baby over to me, and that baby, man, she was just beautiful, with big black eyes and long eyelashes and soft soft skin, so soft it was like what an angel's skin would feel like, and for a second, I could swear that she was looking right at me, looking straight into my soul, and cooing with pleasure, like she knew me and was happy to see me, and I just melted. A moment later, Elizabeth said, "I think I need to change her diaper."

When she came back, she told me what happened.

It started when she started helping Barry out after school, meeting him in his classroom to sort out papers and stuff. Then it was going out for coffee. Then it was going to his house for a quick bite. Her mother was a legal secretary and often had to work late, and her father had died when Elizabeth was little, so she was alone a lot. Barry made her feel special, she said. Chosen. It felt magical to ride along with Barry in his awesomely cool vintage Firebird. "It was silver-green," she said. "So pretty, like the color of the ocean." He wasn't that old, either. It took a long time, months, but finally she had sex with him. But she didn't like it, and she tried to break it off with him, but then he got all weird about her, sending her text messages and emails, pulling her over in the hallway at school, until finally she had to tell her mother, who told the school, who told the police, and the whole thing ended up in court.

"Statutory rape," she said. "That's what they call it. Even though he didn't rape me. I mean, not in the way that most people think about it. Turns out he'd done it to another girl, a girl who'd graduated the year before."

"Is that how you got your scar?" I asked, putting two and two together, and imagining the scene: the teacher, enraged, with a knife in his hand; Elizabeth cowering in a corner; and then—slash. Right across the forehead. The blood. The shock. The pain. But again, she just shrugged. "I ran through a window," she said.

I couldn't take in the meaning of her words. *Ran through a window?* "What?"

"Truthfully, I was lucky, because when I went through that thing, I thought it was an open doorway, so I just slammed right into it, and it crashed into a million pieces. I could have been killed, but I wasn't. All I got was this." She pointed to her forehead. "I'm going to get it fixed, by the way, just as soon as Mom works out all the health insurance. I've already met with one plastic surgeon. I'm going to meet someone else too, in the city, see what she says."

But I was stuck back at the mall. "How'd you manage to run through a window again?"

"I was kind of—stealing—and I was pretty sure a mall cop was coming after me, so I panicked and thought I'd better get out of there, I just didn't notice that there was a plate of glass between me and the sidewalk."

I sat there for a while, looking at my rubbery legs, and trying to put all the pieces together. The whole story disturbed me, made me anxious, itchy. And it wasn't because she had a baby, either. Finally, I realized what was missing, what it was that made the whole story seem so random.

"But you loved him, right? I mean, you were in love with him?" I said, thinking about how I had felt about Sophie—how I still felt about Sophie. If Elizabeth had been in love with her teacher, even if he was older, and even if it was against the law, so what that they had sex? If she loved him—even if she didn't now—the whole story made some kind of sense. Because if she didn't love him, that meant that Elizabeth was just—I don't know what, but it wasn't good. "Did you love him?" I asked one more time.

She made a face. "You're kidding, right?"

"No."

Then she got mad. "Love him? Why would I love him? For one thing, he kind of ruined my life. I mean—I liked him, I guess. At first. I liked the attention. I liked feeling like I was so special. But love him? Jesus Christ, by the second time we did it, it was more like—I didn't hate him, okay? But he totally grossed me out. He had hairy wrists. I felt so dirty. I couldn't wash it off, either. Very Lady Macbeth, I'd take these long long showers. But love him? Dear Jesus, no. He was *old*. He *disgusted* me."

With that, another thought crossed my mind, hitting me like a thunderbolt, like clear vision, so strong that I had to simply blurt it out: "You didn't kill him, did you?"

(Are you still with me, Admissions Committee? Do you see what I'm getting at when I claimed, earlier, that my story was probably a tad bit more out there than the usual tales of getting through difficult parental divorces or overcoming ADHD? To wit: I was pretty sure that my best friend was a teacher-slayer.)

"You did, didn't you?"

Finally, Elizabeth laughed and kept laughing, and I started to feel stupid, and finally she broke into these loud whoops of hilarity, and I began to laugh, too. When we calmed down, she said, "IF ONLY!"

"I'm not 100 percent sure I'm following."

"He was so gross and awful and he just—I mean, I was part of it, but he was just this big fat slime-ball creep who—who *convinced* me. Everyone in town was talking about it. They're probably still talking about it. It was the most exciting thing that ever happened there. And *that's* why I can't have your mother going around snooping into my private business. It was all such a big mess. At least in the end, the judge felt sorry for me and my record was expunged. We're supposed to be starting over, here. Mom's words. Because if this is starting over, I'd really rather not."

"But Elizabeth," I said. "Why don't you just meet my mom and tell her the truth? Sure, she's a huge hover-mother pain in the ass, but she's a good person. And none of it was your fault. You were the *victim*. You were the *kid*. And Mom used to represent all kinds of down-and-outs, single moms, kids in the foster care system. She'd understand. She'd get it. Maybe if one day you could just come over. For a half hour. Just enough to satisfy Mom that you don't pose some risk to my mental health."

"No way!" Elizabeth insisted. "And trust me, no one's mother, no matter how liberal she is, wants her son hanging out with a teen mom with a record. If you tell her anything at all about me, I'm dead meat."

"You think?"

"Just get your mom to back off, okay?" she finally said.

15

Sorry," Mom said the next after-
noon when I explained to her why she had to leave Elizabeth alone,
describing the situation in detail while tactfully leaving out the most
sensitive parts, such as Elizabeth's involvement with her teacher, her
shoplifting habit, how she got her scar, and her baby.

"Come on, Mom. All I'm saying is to back off. Elizabeth's just a kid,
like me. You have no business sniffing into her business."

"As I said," Mom said. "Sorry, but no can do."

"But she's the nicest girl ever. Really. You've just got to believe me
on this, okay? She's like—she's just great, okay?"

But Mom was at her very best, fueled by her sense of outraged over-
protectiveness and fully disposed toward reaching into her legal training.
"Why should I believe anything you say, Josh? Item one: you left the
house last night without telling me you were going out at all."

"I left in the afternoon. It was four o'clock. Not even close to night. And I left you a note."

"A note that said 'back later.' Not good enough."

"God, Mom."

"Item two: you didn't get home until after it was already dark."

"I'm six foot two, Mom. Who's gonna mess with me?"

"Item three: when you got home—*after* dark—you lied and said you were out for a run."

"I didn't lie, Mom. I *was* out for a run."

"Item four: you're prevaricating even now. Having told a half truth, you're continuing to cover up for it, and, item five: even if you had been out for a run, what was I supposed to think? You were gone for *hours*. Think, for once. With your history—*of course* I worried."

"Jesus fucking Christ!"

Voices (little "v"): *Lame! Could you even get any lamer? Waa waa! Why don't you go crying to Athens, little Joshy?*

Shut up!

LAME LAME LAME LAME.

"Think of it from my point of view. From mine and your father's. You have been extremely ill. It's not just my right, but my duty to do what I can to ensure that you continue to get well. Which means that I have a very active stake in who you choose to spend time with. God knows that last time around . . ."

"But Mom!" I now said. "You're just wrong. And you have no right to go around harassing Elizabeth or anyone else. I don't even understand how you could send some social worker over there or whatever she was supposed to have been."

"Is that what Elizabeth told you? That I'd sent a social worker over to her house?"

"Something like that."

"Hmm," Mom said, briefly sinking into thought. "Well, I didn't."

"You sent someone over, though, didn't you?"

There was another pause, while Mom put on her "am ruminating" face. Then she said, "No. I couldn't do that even if I had the power to. But I did hire a private investigator."

"You didn't! You couldn't! Oh God, Mom. What are you trying to do? Ruin my already awful, awful, awful life?"

"Honey, if she's all you say she is, she has nothing to worry about. I'm looking into those three boys who harass you too."

"The insects? Stop! Just let me handle them, okay?"

"Bullying is against the law, honey. I just want the school to enforce the laws."

"You just want to humiliate me. I'm legally an adult!"

"Look, hon. Dad and I have never even met this Elizabeth person. But we do know a few things about her that aren't exactly savory."

"What? Mom! NO! Elizabeth is the kindest and best person there is. And it's not like we're romantic. She's my *friend*."

"So you must not know."

"Know what? That she's got a kid?"

"That too?"

"Oh God." I put my head in my hands, realizing immediately that I'd opened my big mouth for nothing. I was, without a doubt, the biggest idiot in the continental United States. My brain was on fire.

"She's also got a long legal paper trail," Mom said after a little while. "A big mess."

"I know. She told me. Okay? She was the victim, Mom. *She* was the kid. She didn't do anything wrong."

"There was an investigation. Some teacher or something. They hushed it up. But I found out about it. And it was messy."

"DO YOU WANT ME TO KILL MYSELF?" I stood up, pacing and yelling and banging doors and punching the wall, but nothing I did, nothing I said, seemed to make the slightest impression on my mother, who just stood there, with her arms crossed, and a look of worried concern on her cross-etched face.

"Girl's a weirdo."

It was Nate, tripping into the kitchen for his usual pre-dinner snack: an apple, a jar of peanut butter, and a bagel, which he scooped up to take back with him to the TV room.

"Don't eat too much!" Mom yelled at his retreating back. "We're going to eat soon."

"I just had practice. I'm hungry."

I got down on my knees and begged: "You don't know Elizabeth. She's great. She's really great. But she has stuff. A dead father, for one thing. No money, for another. And you could ruin her life. Please, for once, just trust me on this."

She heaved another one of her great big sighs. "Why don't you invite her over here and I can decide for myself? Because honestly, hon, the only thing I want is a chance to talk to her. That's all. Is that so much? Is that too much to ask?"

I didn't answer.

"Am I really being that unreasonable?"

"It's just that she has a baby, Mom—and she can't just come over any old time. The second school is out, she goes home to her baby, so her mother can go out to work. I mean, you of all people should understand that."

"So I'll tell you what, then. Why don't I take you and Elizabeth and Elizabeth's baby out for dinner some time? Wouldn't that be nice? Wouldn't that be a treat?"

Really?

I took the stairs two by two, flung open the door to my bedroom, and lunged for Athens, who spent his days sitting on the armchair in the corner, next to a blue-and-yellow Star of David pillow that my grandmother had needlepointed for me for my bar mitzvah. Because at that moment, I actually *yearned* for him—for his fuzzy, blurry face, for the comforting feel of him in my arms. But he wasn't there.

Athens wasn't under the bed, either. Or in the closet. Or tucked weirdly behind a piece of furniture. Or in the attic. Or anywhere at all.

I ran downstairs.

"I hope you're not still so upset, honey," said my mother. "Dad just got home. Let's have dinner."

"Where's Athens?"

"Your floppy little dog?"

"Where is he? I can't find him."

"I don't know, honey. How should I know?"

"You don't know anything about him?"

"Maybe you left him somewhere. Have you checked in the attic?"

"I went everywhere, including the attic, and including my closet and under the pillows and I can't find him! Did you take him, Mom? Because I swear to you, Mom, if you *took* him—" I was so upset I wanted to hit her. My hands were balling into fists. Sweat was pouring down my ribs. "Because, I swear . . ."

Just then Dad came in. "What's this all about?"

"Josh can't find Athens."

"Calm down, son. What can't you find?"

"Not what, Dad. *Who.* Athens."

Just out of my line of vision Mom was making little hush-now gestures, but Dad must not have picked up on it. "What's this now? *Athens?* Last I heard, Athens was the capital of Greece."

Mom interrupted: "Athens is Josh's stuffed dog. From when he was little."

Dad looked puzzled. "Would someone please fill me in?"

Just then, Mom's hand flew up to her mouth. "Oh my God!"

"You *did* take him."

"No—of course not. But I cleaned out the closets today—all those old coats that everyone's outgrown, sweaters, shirts, mittens. I put every-thing on your chair, honey, and then I bagged everything up, you know, for Goodwill, and—"

"Please tell me this is a joke."

"Dear God, I must have put Athens in the bag with all those old clothes."

"You gave him *away?*"

"I'm so sorry."

"Where, Mom? Where did you take him? We need to go there! We need to go down there now! Now, Mom! Hurry up! We need to go find him!"

"We can't, honey. I took everything to the Goodwill store. It closed two hours ago. But don't worry—they won't have done anything with that stuff yet. I'm sure they haven't. It's probably all in the original bags, sitting in the corner, waiting for someone to go through it."

"no!" I yelled, imagining how, in time, Mom would manage to discover and get rid of my one Sophie photo too, and the next thing I knew, I was putting on my running shoes. Then Nate swung himself into my room, saying, "What's happenin', my man?" and the sight of his smirking smart-ass face just made me nuts, and before I knew it, *pow*, I punched him in the stomach. Not hard. But enough for him let out a little gasp. I grabbed the trophy where I'd hidden my Sophie picture and was out the door, tears and snot running together down my face, mingling with snowflakes, mingling with the icy air. Pounding the pavement and waiting to calm down again, thinking of Sophie and how much I loved her, I remembered how after everyone else was sleeping we would sneak out of our respective cabins to meet at the lake, except—

I couldn't remember meeting her there.

It was just me there, at the lake. I waited for her, waiting for what seemed like hours, but she didn't come. It made me so angry! And then I was in her cabin, shaking her, whispering: Wake up! Wake up! Why didn't you meet me, Sophie? We had a plan, remember? Did you change your mind?

Josh? Is that you, Josh? What are you doing here?

Why didn't you meet me? You were supposed to meet me!

Quiet! You'll wake the other girls up.

Why didn't you meet me? We had a plan.

What plan? I'm confused . . . what are you talking about, Josh?

But Sophie.

Are you sleepwalking, Josh? Because you're not really making a lot of sense.

But you and me—

You really have to go back to your own cabin, Josh.

Why?

I'll take you, okay?

She led me outside. In the gleaming night sky I glanced up and saw the big dipper and the little dipper, all that ancient light dancing on my retinas.

I kissed her there, under the giant sky. She pushed me away.

Huh? I said, lunging for her a second time.

I mean it, Josh. No.

My head and my feet were pounding as all that memory flooded me, how she had said no, how she had said, No no no no NO NO NO NO NO.

Stop it, I tell myself, stop remembering, but I can't stop remembering. NO!

"Meaning?"

I looked around. I was standing on the sidewalk in front of Elizabeth's building, shouting into the darkening sky.

"I heard you yelling. You're going to cause an international event if you don't quiet down. What's going on, mister?"

"I ran here," I said.

"Obviously."

"Something happened."

"Tell me about it inside," she said.

"Okay," I said, returning to reality.

"Do you bring a trophy with you on all your runs?"

I had totally forgotten about the thing, but there it was, clenched in my fist.

"A present," I said, handing it to her.

"Oh, that's just so sweet! I just hope you didn't spend a lot of money on this."

"Well, you know," I said. "Got to treat the ladies right."

I followed her up the stairs to her apartment, where she put the trophy in the corner next to a giant package of diapers, picked up Angela, and said, "What's on your mind?"

16

Everyone says that you can't remember things that happened to you before you were five, but I remember exactly when Nate was born, how right before Dad took Mom to the hospital, he asked old Mrs. Petersen from down the street to watch me until Nana could come over, and how she wouldn't let me have peaches for dessert even though Mom usually did; and then going to the hospital with Nana and seeing the small pink thing wrapped up in a blue blanket, and Mom telling me to be gentle, and Dad telling me not to climb on Mom's lap, or breathe too much on the new baby in case I had a cold, and how Mom ate a turkey sandwich and let me have the Jell-O that came with it. It was red Jell-O, my favorite, only Mom said it was all chemicals and she didn't want any chemicals going into the baby's milk, which confused me, and made Nana and Dad laugh when I asked them about it. And then, later, when they came home, Nate slept in my old crib, only now it was his crib because I had a brand new big-boy bed, with a bright red cover on it that Mom said was very grown-up, and a rail around it to keep me from tumbling out. And then all these people came to our house and the rabbi came and Mom cried and one of the grown-ups gave me a toy truck and people said I was a big brother now. But I didn't really know what all the fuss was about, all over this small sniffling thing that couldn't do anything but cry and poop. And then later Dad was saying, "Hush, shh, you're going to wake the baby," or something like that, and his voice was mixed in with a bad dream and then there were pirates in my room trying to kidnap me, but Dad came in and chased the pirates away.

Mom and Dad both said that I couldn't possibly remember any of this, that I must have heard the stories about when Nate was born so many times that I began to believe they were my own memories, that the big-boy bed didn't come until later, that I was too little to ask Mom about chemicals, that I myself was too little to have all but a rudimentary vocabulary.

But I definitely remember that they made me take Nate with me to birthday parties, saying that there would be other little brothers and sisters there, even though there never were. Sometimes he would crawl into my bed at night and we would play make-believe games about the creatures who lived inside our walls.

I was going to be a professional baseball player, and so was he; I was going to be an astronaut, and so was he; I was going to be a train conductor, and so was he.

Nana came over whenever Mom and Dad went away on vacation, but that hardly ever happened, because mainly when we went on vacation, it would be the four of us, together, at the beach or the mountains, and then Nate and I started to go to summer camps in the summer, and Mom and Dad would travel while we were at camp. Then Nana died, of cancer. All of us cried, but Mom cried the most, and on the night after Nana's funeral, Nate dragged his mattress into my room, so he wouldn't have to sleep alone, and we stayed up half the night talking about Nana, how much we both had loved her. Then I was a junior counselor at camp and Nate was a senior camper, and I met Sophie.

That's how it was. And I was telling all of this to Elizabeth while she held Angela, explaining how weird it was that I could remember all that stuff from when I was little all the way up to the beginning of my (original) last year of high school, but I couldn't remember much about Sophie except for the memory I'd just remembered—that memory of that one weird night at camp. Most of my memories of Sophie were like snatches here and there: her beauty, her soft eyes and curls.

"But you just did remember," Elizabeth pointed out. "You remembered that she pushed you away and said no."

"But I can't really remember anything else. I can't even picture what she looked like."

Whereupon I picked up my running trophy, smashed it against the kitchen floor, and unearthed the photo.

"Here," I said.

"That's her, huh?"

"Sophie."

"And you. When you still had two eyes. And weren't so fat."

"Yeah, well."

"Actually, you've lost so much weight you're beginning to look like this guy again." She nodded toward the picture. "But older. More *weathered*."

"Psychoses will do that to you," I said. "Brings out the rugged, sexy, manly look."

"Works if you work it," she said.

"So you'll keep it for me?"

"The photo?"

"It'll be safe here," I explained, and then, remembering Athens all over again, I burst into tears.

"Dude? What is it?"

"Athens—" I started, and as I blubbered out the story, Angela started crying too: we were a stereo of sound. "Goodness sakes," Elizabeth said, getting up. When she returned she had a bottle for Angela and a glass of milk for me, and after a while we both calmed down.

"Plus I'm beginning to think that Sophie wasn't actually my girlfriend."

"Maybe not," Elizabeth said as she rocked Angela in her arms.

"Just for starters," I said. "She was way out of my league. I mean, just take a look her."

"I'm looking," Elizabeth said, gazing at the photo.

"Beautiful, right?"

"Not really."

"Are you *blind*?"

"I have twenty-twenty vision," she said. "But unless this is a really bad picture of her, I'd have to say that Sophie's not going to win the Miss America contest any time soon."

"Are you kidding?"

"Sorry," she said. "But she's—she's not really all that great. If you want my opinion, I'd say she's pretty average."

I honestly didn't know how Elizabeth of all people could say that *Sophie* was average in the looks department. But as Elizabeth continued to rock Angela, I began to see something I had never noticed before. Elizabeth had a radiance and delicacy about her, but you had to notice it to notice it. As I noticed it, I noticed something else, coming from inside me. It was love. Not the love I felt for Sophie, though. The love I had for Elizabeth was quiet and simple, almost as if she were Buster, but not, because Buster was a dog whereas Elizabeth—Elizabeth was my friend.

I shrugged and said, "My mom is dead set on meeting you."

"This is truly not a good idea." Elizabeth sounded miserable. "The whole idea is that no one knows where I live, or about Angela, or any of it. If it gets out that we've moved to New Jersey, the creep could find me and get obsessed with me again. He'll be out of prison soon."

"In that case . . ." I was thinking aloud. "Maybe you need a body guard. You have to admit that, if nothing else, I'm big."

"Great plan, Batman," Elizabeth said.

"But what if he comes after you?"

"I don't know," she said. "I'm already the teen skank redneck hick weirdo of Western High. All I need is for people to find out about Angela, and I'll really be popular."

I looked at her. She looked at me. The baby gurgled. Then we were laughing our heads off, laughing so hard that the new tears washed all the old ones away.

"Can I sleep over?" I said.

17

When I called to tell her that I was staying at Elizabeth's, Mom said that if I didn't come home, she'd send the cops out after me, but when I lied and told her that Elizabeth's mother would be home by six, she calmed down, or at least calmed down enough not to call the cops, though I suspect that she probably drove by Elizabeth's house a couple of times anyway, just to make sure that I hadn't burned down the building, or whatever. After my run, I was too tired to worry about it, and I fell into the bed that Elizabeth made for me on the sofa like I was already unconscious. But without Athens, I couldn't quite fall into a deep sleep, and I tossed and turned trying to get comfortable. Around midnight, Elizabeth's mother tip-toed in, and once or twice during the night I heard the baby cry and Elizabeth getting up to comfort her. In the morning, I met Elizabeth's mother, who had quick, darting movements like a bird's, and eyes so dark they looked black. She made us eggs and toast, chatting away in a Southern accent about how breakfast was the most important meal of the day, but by then I was so bleary from lack of sleep that the eggs tasted like yellow cardboard and the toast like gray cardboard. But I sure liked Elizabeth's mother, and I liked being there, at Elizabeth's house, eating breakfast with them. "And I want you to know," Elizabeth's mother said, "you're welcome here at our house anytime. Anytime, you hear me?"

I wanted to crawl into her lap and stay there for the rest of my life.

Instead, I had to go to school, where—wait for it—Mom was waiting for me. She had positioned herself just outside the principal's office, which, because the principal's office is just off to the side from where you enter the building, meant that she had an uninterrupted view of all the kids coming in and there was no escaping her. Elizabeth herself had just enough time to make a getaway before Mom, spotting me, wove her way through the mass of kids, throwing her arms around me and hugging me so tightly that I could feel all her small bones. "I'm going to Goodwill right now," she said. "I want you to know that, Josh. I'll be there at nine exactly, when it opens. I'll be the first one there. I'm going to find Athens. I promise."

"Okay," I mumbled.

"I'm just so sorry, Josh," she said. "Are you okay?"

"Tired," I said.

She eyed me suspiciously, as if she expected to find some contraband on my person, or perhaps some other sign of Elizabeth's malignant influence.

"And Elizabeth?" she said. "Was that your friend Elizabeth?"

"Who?"

"The girl you came in with."

"Yes."

"She's a little thing, isn't she?"

"She's not what you'd call plus size."

"I mean, she's really, *really* small. I didn't know she was such a bitty thing. You must be twice her size."

"Your point?"

Ignoring me, Mom said, "Where'd she go?"

"Uh. Class?"

"Because Josh," she said, her voice cast low, "that girl. Honey, I really don't think you should be spending time with her. Let alone staying over at her house."

"Her mom was home. Plus she has a baby, as you well know. I mean, what kind of trouble could we get into? Get *cried* to death? Poisoned by diaper poop?"

"I almost called the police last night, to come and get you."

"You already told me."

"But what I didn't tell you was the reason I didn't. It was because Nate, of all people, talked me out of it. He said that, in his opinion, your friend is weird, but not dangerous. Your father agreed. But I couldn't sleep, not a wink."

"That makes two of us."

"God knows what goes on in that household, Josh. I really hate to be the one to break it to you, but your friend Elizabeth has quite a paper trail, a record, even."

"She doesn't have a record, Mom," I said. "That's just not true. It was *expunged*." I felt clever, using the legal term.

"Except it is true, Josh! Or at least the things she did are true—that she did them. Good God, sweetheart! I know it's tough for you—being here, in high school again. And in your little brother's class. And having to do senior year all over again. And, well, *everything*. But with your background, what you've done . . ."

"What have I done?"

Mom blanched. And when I say "blanched," I mean it in its most literal-descriptive way: "Make white or pale by extracting color."

"What have I *done*, Mom?"

"Enough, Josh. Right now, I have to put my foot down, that's what! No more Elizabeth! Not unless I know for a fact that she's not dangerous for you." Her voice was loud now, so loud that kids were looking at us, so loud that I felt like I'd felt in the first grade when, during the winter seasonal holiday pageant, in which I played a pine tree, I was so nervous about remembering my one line ("I'm an evergreen so I keep my needles green") that I peed in my pants.

Inside my brain was complete chaos, complete darkness. I could feel the blood pumping in my limbs and in my veins and into the ventricles of my brain stem. The bell rang for the start of first period and I turned and walked away.

Halfway up the stairs to the third floor, I lost it. And when I say *lost it,* I exaggerate not. It wasn't just rage pushing up in me, or fear, or shame, or sadness or anguish or hate, but some giant combo platter, all mixed in with Athens. The next thing I knew, I was on the landing where the stairs turned, looking out the window, rocking back and forth, and crying. Kids were rushing past me, and all I could think of was how nice it would be to jump out the window onto the parking lot below. The drop was thirty feet, maybe forty.

Smack.

It would be easy.

I stared at the drop—how long would it take?

"Think we should call the nurse?"

"He's crying—"

A pat on my shoulder. "Hey. You okay?" A girl's voice. "Want me to get you some water or something?"

"No."

"Hey, big guy." Another voice.

"Please just leave me alone."

"You look really upset, is all. Come on, let me help you."

"Go away."

"Hey man," said another voice I didn't recognize.

"We need to get someone to help him."

"Someone get a teacher."

"Josh? Come on, man . . ."

"Dude?"

Elizabeth's voice floated toward me through time and space.

"Josh? Josh? Can you hear me?"

Then she was right there, right up in my face, then right up in my chest, strapping herself in-between me and the window pane. I could see the top of her head, the places where her part was crooked, the fishy whiteness of her scalp, and the place where her scar made bumps under her hair.

"Let's get you out of here," she said. Then she pressed herself against me and away from the window, her face wetting my shirt.

"Why are *you* crying?" I finally said, coming to, as if out of a trance. "I'm the one who lost Athens."

"You're not the only one who's lost stuff."

"Mom says I can't see you anymore," I said. "She says we can't be friends."

"She's wrong, though," Elizabeth said.

"What if Athens is really lost?"

"He isn't," Elizabeth said. "Your mom will find him."

"What if she can't?"

"She will."

18

But Elizabeth was wrong.

Mom just about committed hara-kiri, apologizing, but no amount of telephoning and looking for Athens helped. He was gone. *Gone* gone. Vanished. Without a trace. Like Sophie. Except of course, in the case of Athens, I at least knew what had happened to him, more or less: he'd been thrown out, and was now moldering at the bottom of a giant pile of New Jersey garbage, or he was a nest for rats, or had been torn into a hundred pieces of old fluff in a shredding machine. One way or another, he was never put on a shelf for someone to take home with him, which I knew because I myself went down to the Goodwill store and the only stuffed animals they had were new or brand-new, some with the tags still on them. I tried not to think about him too much, but it was hard. Even Dr. Rose, who usually wanted to focus on my dreams, daydreams, voices, appetite, memory, reflexes, sleeping habits, and/or lack thereof, spent a whole session with me on Athens alone, saying how sorry he was, nodding his head in sympathy, reaching out to touch the top of my hand and assuring me that despite everything, I was getting better.

Then there was the whole matter of Elizabeth and how my mother was trying to kill the one friendship I had but I ran out of time before I could even get to that and didn't know what Dr. Rose could do for me in any case, not in terms of my mother's extremist nut-job views on the matter, and they said that *I* was the one with mental health issues when I was beginning to think that the real psycho in the family wasn't me at all, except of course that it had been me, and not Mom, who had considered how nice it would be to fly off the GW Bridge, and now I couldn't remember any of the really important things that had happened during my tenure as Superjosh. By the end of the session, I was exhausted from crying. Dr. Rose did something he never did. He hugged me.

"You're doing good," he said. "Believe it or not, all of this, including the misery, is part of the healing process."

"Then why do I feel like shit?"

"I know it's hard. But you're getting healthier every day."

A week or so later—just in time for Hanukkah—I got my new eyeball. It took an hour or two working with the eyeball technician before I could get it in and out without difficulty, but once I got the hang of it, it was no big deal. It looked pretty good, too: not like my real eye, because it didn't move back and forth and has this weird glassy sheen, but at last I could lose the eye patch. And because I'd been running, I'd lost some weight, too, enough that my clothes were beginning to get loose on me. Enough that I no longer looked like a monster.

It didn't make up for the loss of Athens, though, so even with my new eyeball and my newfound nonfatness and the fact that despite everything, Elizabeth and I continued to hang out, Hanukkah was dreary. Outside, it was cold, wet, raw, and colorless, with unbearably lonely shadows. Inside, we treated each other warily. The lights were lit; the songs were sung; but it was all done as if by a grouping of robots. As we opened our presents, the only people in the room who seemed excited were the cats, who rubbed themselves up against us over and over again, as if expecting to get presents of their own, and Buster, who thumped his tail wildly at the mere mention of his name.

Mom and Dad gave me a gift certificate to the Running Shop along with an Asics beanie, lightweight running gloves, and thermals—everything but the shoes, which I had to try on in person. It was a nice present, actually pretty much the best thing I could think of other than finding Athens. Nate gave me a framed picture of himself, running, but I couldn't tell if it was meant to be a joke or not. "Thanks, dude," I told him. "Thanks, Mom and Dad," I said, meaning it. "You didn't have to give me all this stuff, you know."

They gave Nate pretty much the same thing, except without the gift certificate because he already had running shoes, and I gave Nate a twenty-dollar gift certificate for iTunes, which I paid for from my ancient if diminished stash of bar mitzvah money. Nate fidgeted around with his cell phone, glancing at the screen, pressing buttons.

"Thanks," Nate said, actually looking up from his cell phone.

Mom said, "What a thoughtful, thoughtful gift, Josh."

And Nate said, "What about me? I gave him something too."

"If you can call it a gift. You didn't even buy that frame."

"Of course I bought the frame, Mom."

"Funny, because I had the exact one in a box in the basement. You know, where I keep things we don't use any more."

And we all just sat there, not saying or doing anything, until Mom got up to clear away the torn-up wrapping paper.

One morning a few days after we'd gotten out of school for the holidays, Elizabeth called me and said she wanted me to take her to the city, that she'd never been, that her mother could watch Angela, and that if I didn't take her it was all over between us etcetera, only of course she was just joking about that last bit because she knew that I knew that she knew that we were each other's only real friends. The real problem was that as far as my mother was concerned, the no-Elizabeth rule still held.

"I'm going out for a run!" I yelled as I slammed the front door behind me and then skedaddled down the street. Ten minutes later, I was waiting with Elizabeth for the NJ Transit train to Penn station—the same train, by the way, that I used to take when I went to visit Sophie at NYU—and a half hour later we were gazing out the train's dirty smudged windows as we choo-chooed over the Meadowlands. Five minutes after that I texted Mom that I was going into the city with a friend and to not worry (ha ha ha ha) and an hour after that, Elizabeth and I were sitting in Washington Square, eating soft pretzels. It was Elizabeth's idea, going to NYU, because, first off, she had decided that if she won the lottery, that's where she wanted to go to college, and, second off, she thought that if I saw the place again it would jog my memory. But nothing came to me except what I already knew, which was that I loved Sophie, and she loved me—except maybe not. The only thing I knew for sure was that I used to come here, to visit her.

It was cold. Dark gray cold, the kind with icicles. The kind that makes everyone look like they're wearing black, even if they're not.

"So?" Elizabeth said.

"Nothing."

"Nothing at all?"

"No memories of what happened, if that's what you mean."

"Then what?"

"Just Athens," I said, beginning to feel tears line up behind my eyeballs and clog up my throat again. "He was—he was kind, that's what he was. I know it sounds stupid, but he had these understanding eyes, and this sweet expression on his face. I wasn't the only person who saw it, either, how kind his face was. He was just—*kind*."

Nate and I used to play this slightly sick game called "What would you do in the Holocaust?" And we'd make up different scenarios: If your mother was being pushed into the gas chamber but you had a chance to escape, would you? If you had to crawl on your belly through the sewer to escape from the ghetto even if it meant leaving your family behind, would you do that too? If you had to either kill someone else or be killed yourself, which would you choose? What if the someone else were a little kid? What if it was your own grandmother? The game never included any mention of how hard it would be to exist in Auschwitz without your favorite stuffed animal.

"On the other hand," she said, "you do have me."

I didn't say anything. I was thinking about how Mom was so far up my butt that she was like a permanent wedgie.

"I've decided that if it's so effing important for your mother, I'll come over to your house," she continued. "If your mom is set on ruining my life, she'll ruin it anyway. But at least, I don't know—at least we can still be friends. Once she sees I'm not a murderer. Or whatever it is she thinks I've done."

"What made you change your mind?"

"Mom thinks I should," she said as we watched a flock of black birds land on the pavement in a flapping flutter of wings.

The night before school started up again, Nate knocked on my door. "Need to talk to you, bro."

"What?"

"I know how you lost your eye."

I was reading *The Great Gatsby*, a book I'd read before, and hated. I hated it this time just as much. Stupid, boring, snobby, spoilt people. Stupid green light. Stupid English 12 Honors. So I was already in a bad mood.

"Thanks for the perverted joke."

"I mean it."

"Very funny. Plus, as you can see," I said, pointing to my new glass orb, "it's been found."

"No, really. I know what happened. But if Mom and Dad find out that I told you they will kill me. I mean it, Josh."

Finally, I registered the meaning of his words, except, of course, I didn't completely. The one thing I picked up on was that what I'd suspected had been right all along: my parents, and possibly my many doctors, had known all along, but wouldn't tell me. But they'd told Nate. And now Nate was about to tell me what I pretty much already knew: namely, that in some gesture of pure insanity, I'd poked out my own eye. Maybe with a knife. Maybe with a fireplace poker. Maybe with a screwdriver. In the end, the tool of choice wouldn't much matter, but at least I'd finally know for sure that I'd done it to myself.

"I won't tell Mom and Dad."

"Look," he continued, dragging the words out slowly, as if he'd been planning this little scene in his mind and had decided to string it out as long as possible in order to wring maximum torture out of it. "It's not nice."

"What *happened*?"

"You sure you want to know?"

"Of course I'm sure."

"And you won't let anyone know I told you, right? I mean, seeing that I'm already in the crap box, parental-wise."

"Just say it."

"You really mean it? That you won't tell that I told?"

"Fuck you, Nate. I already said so, didn't I? And anyway, I'm pretty sure that you're going to tell me that I did it myself."

"What?"

"That that's the big secret: I did it to myself. You yourself once almost let the cat out of the bag, and—"

But he cut me off: "Sophie did it."

I almost laughed. Then when I saw how quiet and serious he'd become, with no sign whatsoever of his usual, laugh-a-minute self, I merely said, "You're lying."

"That's what happened. That's why they won't tell you. Because it was Sophie."

"That makes no sense," I said.

"Listen," he said, his voice dropping so low as he sat next to me on the bed in the place where Athens used to sit that I could barely make out the meaning of his words. "They think that if you found out, things would be even worse—that you'll lose what's left of your nut."

But my mind was swirling too much to translate his words into coherent thoughts.

"They're still not sure you're okay."

"Duh."

"I mean, you're not going to go out and do something crazy now that I've told you, right?"

I thought about it, it's the truth, because the way I felt, the idea of going for a nice long rest on the train tracks had a certain appeal. But then I thought of Elizabeth. And then I thought that I didn't actually want to die. And then I said, "Probably not."

"Probably not? Please, Josh. Listen—God, I'm a moron. I shouldn't have told you! Jesus, how stupid can you be?" He just sat there, breathing really hard, like someone had just beaten him up, his eyes filming over with wetness. Then he smacked himself.

"Don't," I said.

"I'm sorry. I shouldn't have told you."

"But why would Sophie do that to me? It just doesn't make any sense. And how do you even know? You never even met her."

"Sorry, bro, but that's really all I know. She stabbed you—somehow. At her dorm, I think, but even that, I'm not sure of. Mom and Dad won't talk about it. They say it's all highly confidential, that their lawyers advised them not to talk about it. Stuff like that."

"Their lawyers?"

"I don't know, Josh. All I know is from overhearing them—at first when you were first found. Someone called 911 and they took you to the emergency room. In the city, because that's where it happened. That's when I heard Mom tell Dad that Sophie had done it to you."

I thought about punching his face in, but then I realized he'd already done the job for me, and then I realized that Nate had been taking punches all along.

"With what?"

"What do you mean?"

"What did she stab me with? A knife? A piece of glass? What?"

"How would I know?"

"But you have to know." It was all I could do to keep my voice from staying inside my throat, from not leaping out of my body and filling the whole world with screams.

"The only other thing I know is that you'd gone AWOL. You used to do that all the time. Go to the city. Freak everyone out."

"I did that all the time?"

"All the freaking time, man," he said. "It really sucked, too, being the only kid around here."

"And you're sure?"

"You've got to believe me!" And now he *was* crying, a rare display of any emotion other than indifference. "I'm already persona-non-person as far as they're concerned. If they knew I told you . . ." Then little brother actually lowered his head into his hands, smacking himself with his open palms until I took his two hands in mine and, pulling them toward me, told him to take it easy.

So I tried to remember. I tried and tried and tried to remember. I closed my eye(s) and tried to remember Sophie taking a knife—or a rock, or a piece of glass—and stabbing me in the eyeball. But I couldn't. All I could remember was how much I had loved her. And then I remembered something else, and it was weird, too, because when I remembered this new memory, I realized that I had never not remembered it, that it had always been there, kind of crouching, like a kid playing hide-and-seek behind a sofa only the sofa isn't pushed against a wall so all you have to do is look his way and there he is, gotcha. And what I re-remembered was that I *had* gone to NYC one day—it was a different time from when I tried to run there, because, first of all, it was warm, as warm as summer though the trees had begun to yellow, and second of all, I'd come in on the bus. It was a weekend. I thought I would surprise her. But I couldn't find her, and they wouldn't let me into the library to look for her, and when I knocked on her door at her dorm no one answered, and she wouldn't answer her phone or text me back, so I decided to wait for her at the door to her dorm room. I waited and waited. I fell asleep waiting. My cell phone kept ringing: Mom, Dad, Mom, Dad, Mom, Dad. I didn't pick up.

I drifted off to sleep, wrapped up in Sophie.

"Get up." When my eyes adjusted I saw Sophie standing over me.

"What are you doing here?"

I rubbed my eyes. I sat up. "I came to see you."

"No, Josh. You can't do this. You have to go home."

"Why didn't you answer your phone? Why aren't you returning my emails? Sophie—I love you, Sophie. You and I: we're meant to be together. We're like—I don't know. We're like, magic or something. You're magic. Please. It's hard for me to explain."

"Leave. Now. Just leave."

"We've been joined together by the universe," I said, and as I said it, I knew it was true.

It was beyond love, what I felt for Sophie. It was more like she was me. Her lips, her eyes, her wonderful skin and soft soft hair . . .

"I love you."

"You're scaring me."

"I'll never leave you."

"I'm calling the campus police."

The next thing I knew, I was being hauled out of there, and then I was on the street, and then I was sitting looking out the window of the bus, heading for New Jersey, or at least I think that's where it was going. I must have gotten home somehow, too, because I didn't see Sophie for a while after that. Or did I?

19

"Nate told me how I lost my eye," I told Elizabeth in school the next day before telling her exactly what he'd told me, after which she yawned, scratched under her left armpit, and in a tone that conveyed complete what's-the-big-deal-ness, said, "Do you believe him?"

It hadn't occurred to me not to believe him. "Well, yeah. I do, absolutely. The way he told me—there was no way he was making it up."

"But you personally can't remember it?"

"I just can't. I keep trying to remember, but the actual thing itself— nothing. Just a big blank of nothing where my eye used to be."

"What about your parents? Did you ask them?"

"I don't want to get Nate in trouble. You know how my mother is."

"Well, yeah," she agreed, scratching again, this time the right armpit. "Your mother is also an undeniable truth not to be denied."

"So when do you want to come over and meet the fam?"

"Uh. Never?"

"But you said you would."

"True."

"So you will?"

"Guess I have to."

"And another thing?" I said.

She raised her eyebrows.

"Sophie didn't even like me. Not even a little bit. I mean, maybe she did, at first, when we met at summer camp. But then—I must have been stalking her. I went to NYU this one time to see her and she was like get the effing eff out of here you effing hole butt douchebag nitwit turd wad or I will call the effing cops and have your fat sorry sagging butt dragged off to jail."

"In those words exactly?"

"That's what it felt like," I said.

"And did she?"

"Did she what?"

"Have your fat sorry sagging butt dragged off to jail?"

"No," I said. "But she did call the campus police."

"You must have scared the shit out of her."

"I must have," I said.

Two days later, Elizabeth and Angela came over for dinner.

Beforehand, Mom was like: "What do you think she'd like to eat does she eat meat oh what am I saying your dad's off meat well do you think she'd like salmon and some simple vegetables and a salad or maybe I should just make a huge salad, with bread and cheese that kind of thing?"

And I was like: "I really don't think Elizabeth cares."

And she was like: "Because I'm such a monster that just so long as I don't eat her alive, it doesn't matter what I serve, right?"

And I was like: "God, Mom, really?"

The good news, if you could call it good news, was that in all the stupidosity over Elizabeth, Mom had kind of forgotten about the trio of singing insects, which by then were a non-entity, non-issue anyway, as they had kind of disappeared into the great unwashed non-shaving boner-champ jerkoff-generals of the freshman class. In other words, they left me alone. The bad news was that by the time Elizabeth showed up, Mom had worked herself up into such a pitch of hyped-up joviality that it was like watching a really really really bad sitcom from the eighties.

Mom, too cheerily: "So YOU'RE Elizabeth! So nice to meet you at last! So really really really great! So glad you could come!"

"Hello, Mrs. Cushing. Hello, Mr. Cushing."

"And you and Josh have become such good friends! Well, isn't that just so wonderful! I've made vegetarian lasagna for dinner! It used to be Josh's favorite!" (Which it wasn't.) "Now that Josh's father is going health-food on us, well, you know. There's no such thing as eating too healthfully. Ha ha! I do hope you like vegetarian lasagna, Elizabeth! Do you?"

"It smells delicious."

Looking at me and Nate and Dad, as all three of us froze in WTF-ness, Mom said: "You boys don't mind if Elizabeth and I have a little chat? Girl to girl? Girl talk? If you know what I mean?"

Dad: "Sure, honey. Um . . . see you in a minute, okay, Elizabeth?"

Elizabeth, sending death ray eyes to me: _____.

Me, under my breath, to Nate: "What's Mom doing?"

Nate: "Beats *moi*."

Angela: "Waa waa waa."

Elizabeth: "Excuse me, Mrs. Cushing, but I think Angela needs to be changed."

Mom: "I'll help!"

Elizabeth: "I guess I'll use the bathroom . . . ?"

Mom: "Right up the stairs, dear, let me show you."

And they go upstairs, and a second later I can hear Angela screaming, and a moment after that I myself am on the landing around the corner from the bathroom, eavesdropping.

"I understand you've had a whole world of trouble," said my mother.

"Yes, ma'am."

"And you came here, to New Jersey, to start over. Or at least that was one of your reasons?"

"Yes, ma'am."

"Even though the man who hurt you—I understand he went to prison?"

"Ma'am? Is there something you want to ask me outright?"

"No, Elizabeth," my mother said. Then, through the crack in the door, I saw something I didn't think I'd see. My mother was bowing her head, taking Elizabeth's two hands in hers, and in a very quiet voice, a voice so low it was almost a whisper, she said, "Do you understand how sick Josh has been? How sick he still is?"

"I'm pretty sure he's filled me in."

"But are you aware that he may not always be in control of himself—of his actions?"

"He's told me a lot of stuff, Mrs. Cushing. Everything, really."

"And you know what he did?"

"He's told me everything."

"Did he—the father of your child—do that to you?"

"Do what?"

"Your scar," I heard Mom say. "Did he—did he *hurt* you?"

But instead of hearing Elizabeth's answer, all I heard was a wail, and then a shriek, as Angela kicked into full-scale baby-crying. Then she calmed down. Then nothing.

There was total silence as I slowly realized what was really going on here. Mom was warning Elizabeth to stay away from me.

20

After that, for a day or two or maybe it was three, I can't remember exactly, but the point is: Elizabeth disappeared. She wasn't at school. She didn't answer her phone or return my text messages, except once when I texted her to ask her if she was still my friend and she texted back: *Chill, I'm busy.* But she wasn't at her house when, in desperation, I ran there, and she wasn't there the next time I ran there either. I was so distraught that when Dr. Rose suggested that I go back to my TITSS meetings, I agreed.

"Oh, honey, things will look up," said my mother, the author of the ruination of my life, as she dropped me off.

As I made my way down the stairs to the ground level where our meetings were held, I itched for a cigarette, but then I remembered that since I'd started running I'd kind of stopped smoking, a big problem, given that I was doing what I was about to do: facing a meeting without smokes. When I got there, the room was already crowded, with the usual array of the gray-skinned and the scarred, the tormented and the tortured, the obese, the merely fat (me), and the anorexic.

"So," Fleur said immediately, before even launching into the meeting opening, and without even glancing my way. "I'm afraid I have bad news."

"Bring it on," said a kid with chartreuse green hair and a swastika tattooed on his wrist.

"Well, I don't know how to say it without just saying it. So here-a-goes." But then she didn't say a word. Not a single word. Not one. *Tick, tick, tick*, the moments ticked by. Finally she came out with it.

"Susan has committed suicide."

"No, she didn't," some nitwit said.

"I'm so sorry to have to just blurt it out like this," Fleur continued. "It's just so—awful. So awful and so shocking. But I want you to know, I want all of you to know, that suicide is not, by any measure, your fate, too. What Susan did was Susan's choice, and hers alone."

Dramatic to the end, she did it on Christmas day, dousing herself with kerosene and lighting herself on fire on the front yard of her parents' red-brick colonial in West Orange, in a display of true pyrotechnics that no doubt lit up the entire neighborhood and thus made the festive day even more festive. Which is not how Fleur put it. She merely said, "Fire. She burned herself to death."

While Fleur spoke, the rest of us, the non-dead and so-far-non-suicidal, looked down at the floor and tried not to completely freak out. Because if Susan could do it, then why not the funny little red-headed dork sitting to my right or the pretty girl with the long braid sitting next to Fleur or, for that matter, me?

"We need to work this through, to unpack this, to process this, as a group," Fleur said.

Nobody said anything.

"We need to feel our feelings," Fleur said. "To mourn the fact that one of us didn't make it. That the loss of one of us scars all of us."

And there it was, that word, *scar*—which made me think of Elizabeth' scar, and that other scar, that other girl who had a scar, whose scar—

". . . and when any one of us suffers, we all feel it . . ."

The words batting around in my head, I was so furious I thought I was going to explode. *Why'd you scare her off like that Mom what did I do that was so terrible you made her afraid of me my only friend first Athens and now Elizabeth and oh God Mom really I may as well be dead really really I didn't put that scar there it was an accident, she stepped through a plate-glass window.*

". . . and I can only imagine that every person here is as bewildered, frightened, and plain old freaked out as I am, possibly other feelings as well, which we need to explore, together, here, where it's safe."

Meantime, I sat there, continuing to have a huge argument in my head with my mother, when this kid with major braces stood up and, in a voice so pissed off that I returned to reality, said, "But you're not one of us. You're normal."

Fleur nodded, neither in agreement nor dismissal.

"And who are you to tell us that we need to mourn?" the kid continued. "Susan was a bitch."

"She was ill," Fleur finally said. "Very, very ill."

"She was a true bitch," the kid said.

"She really was," said the girl with the braid down her back. "She used to text all this shit to me, she called me—I don't even want to say it."

"She did that to me, too," said a second girl.

"Me, too."

"I hate to say it, but I kind of fucking hated her fucking guts."

And so forth and so on it went, a chorus of how hard it was to feel sad for a girl whose sole purpose seemed to be to make you feel like shit, while I realized two things simultaneously. The first was that, obviously, I wasn't the only one Susan tormented. The second: the girl didn't have any friends. None. Zero. Nada. No one. Whereas I—

I texted Elizabeth immediately, to tell her the latest. But she didn't respond except to say *Ugh.* I texted back *That's all you can say?* and this time she didn't even respond with an emoji. Finally I understood: Mom had gotten to her and she was letting me down gently. She wanted out of my life; she wanted to be as disappeared as Sophie was.

I told Dr. Rose about Sophie, how she had never loved me, how I must have scared the living shit out of her, and about Nate, what he had told me about my eye, and about Susan, and he said that I was doing good work. I told him about Elizabeth and he nodded his head. I told him that Mom had finally achieved her goal of driving her out of my life, and he stroked his chin and asked me why I was so sure. I told him that I missed Athens, and he said that he knew I did. I told him that I missed Athens so much it was like someone had carved a hole in my heart, and he said that he understood. I told him that as much as I loved Athens, I loved Elizabeth even more.

I told him that I felt like an imposter, that I was merely playing a role, that I had put on a Josh Cushing costume and had learned to imitate his voice so well that no one could tell the difference.

Dr. Rose said that the feeling would pass. He said that as I became more and more stable, I'd be able to tolerate my anxiety with greater and greater equanimity.

Again I texted Elizabeth, telling her how a part of me was glad that Susan was dead, and again Elizabeth didn't respond, until, two days later, she sent an entire word: *Sorry*. Then Mom and Dad sat me down in the living room and with great solemnity told me that they knew I was hurting, but that it would pass, that Elizabeth had her own life to live, as did I. "You can still see her in school," they said. "We're not trying to break up your friendship, just put boundaries around it. For both your sakes."

I just sat there, dumb and blind with pain.

"Is there anything you want to tell us?" they finally said, and I looked up, at these people I barely knew, opened and closed my mouth like a fish, and, later that night, lit my bed on fire.

21

Oops.

I know: not funny, right? And it wasn't. And I didn't mean to do it. It was, I tried to explain, a *side effect*. An unwarranted, unplanned consequence of my attempt to quell the deeper pain inside me. A poor choice, if you will—perhaps even a disastrous one. But not a failed suicide. Not even a suicide attempt. Because frankly, if I were to do suicide, I'd do it right. Whereas all I did was decide to calm my nerves with a cigarette or two or three, the remainder of my go-to-emergency pack that I'd had the foresight to hide months earlier, after Mom found my first hiding place, and the next thing I knew, an ashy spark fell on my bedsheet and . . . *whoosh!*

Just like Susan, as Dr. Rose and others eventually pointed out, only not.

And anyway, the burns weren't all that bad, though they looked pretty disgusting. They did kind of cover half my body, but they were mainly just cosmetic, surface-of-the-surface only, such that rather than be roasted, I was merely toasted.

This is totally in retrospect, though, because at the time, covered in silver oxide and bandages that the nurses had to change twice a day, my entire body was engulfed in pain. It hurt worse than anything I could have imagined, ever. It hurt like poison, like snakebite, like cancer, like glass, like fire.

I could smell my own flesh, how it smelled like hamburger.

I had to stay in the hospital for almost a week, with no visitors other than Mom and Dad, who came wearing surgical masks and sterile gloves because of risk of infection.

But even with their faces hidden, I could tell that this time, I'd *really* done it. Even if I hadn't nearly killed myself, I'd nearly killed them. And saying "sorry," which I did a few thousand times, didn't seem to soften the look on Mom's face that I could see even with the mask on: the frightened eyes, the sharp darts of worry lines that spread from the far corners of her eyes all the way to her hair line. Dad's voice was pitched so low that it was as if he was afraid he'd kill me with unintentionally high decibel levels. On the phone, Nate told me how bad things were at home, and I felt even worse, but even he wasn't allowed in to see me. Too many germs.

"I promise you," I'd say. "It was a mistake. I didn't mean to do it. I promise you that I'm not trying to kill myself. I'm just so so sorry."

"Oh, Josh . . ."

To this day I don't know how Elizabeth managed to sneak in after visiting hours were over, carrying a medium-sized stuffed rabbit, because, as she put it when she handed it to me, "The last thing you need is an Athens-almost-ran."

The rabbit was brown, floppy, and soft, like he/she'd been prehugged.

"Where were you? Why didn't you return my calls? Why didn't you text me?"

"You're welcome," she said.

"Seriously, where were you?"

"I brought you a present," she said. "And risked my reputation as a law-abiding visitor of hospitals to do so. And all you can say is *Where were you?*"

We stared at each other.

"Thank you."

"Any time."

"You disappeared," I said again. "And I couldn't find you. I thought you'd dumped me. I was pretty sure Mom had gotten to you and you'd dumped me and I'd never see you again."

"Chillax," she said. "Why would I dump you?"

"Because you're scared of me?"

"Just because you were, you know, kind of psychotic?"

"That would be one reason."

"Any others?"

"Then where'd you go?" I said, sounding whiny and pathetic and somewhat less than intelligent even in my own ears. It was dark in the room, lit only by the weird green light leaking in from the hall. How could she have just bailed on me like that? "I thought you'd left New Jersey to get away from me. And your text messages were so—abrupt. Like you were giving me the brush-off."

"Aren't you the drama queen?" she said, rolling her eyes. "I just had to go back home to do some legal stuff. Boring as all get-out, too. And really depressing and awful too. And did I mention how awful and depressing it was? Like: ugh. People kept staring at me, like I was the *numero uno* attraction at the youth-goes-astray-and-triumphs-over-evil freak show. We were there to deal with money. Mom sued the county, over letting a sexual predator teach in the public schools because as it turned out my teacher hadn't just gone after this other girl who was a few years ahead of me, but he'd done the same thing to some girls in another state—Texas, I think. The good news is that we actually got a little money, which means that I can get my scar fixed. Because, you know, plastic surgery is *expensive* and even with insurance, me and Mama aren't exactly swimming in money."

I held the funny little rabbit in my two giant hands, holding him out before me so I could get a good look. I liked him right away, partly because of his floppy ears, partly because the expression on his bunny face was kind. "I'm glad," I said.

"What are you going to call him?" She whispered even though no one else was in the room.

"Elizabeth the Second," I said. "I think she's a she."

"No, really."

I shrugged. "Or maybe Leo."

"I like Leo."

"Susan killed herself."

"I know."

"What do you mean, you know? How could you know?"

"You texted me, remember? Plus your brother told me."

"How'd *he* know?"

"Everyone knows, that's how. It was in the papers. It isn't every day that a girl lights herself on fire in her parents' front yard."

"Why didn't you text back?"

"First, I did, or at least I did once, and second, since when are you a copycat?"

"It was an accident."

"You look like raw meat."

"So you can only imagine how dandy I feel."

"Listen," she said. "Never mind. I'll tell you later. Someone's coming. I don't want to get in even more trouble than I'm already in, and if they find me here after hours . . ."

"Oh, come on," I said. "Just tell me."

"Next time."

But there was no next time, and that's because Mom got wind of Elizabeth's nighttime visit and absolutely positively forbade me from seeing her, talking to her, texting her, emailing her and so forth, which of course was impossible, but seeing that I was an invalid and extremely tired and on doctor's orders to stay home, she managed to put the kibosh on Elizabeth anyway, which was tantamount to my truly having no reason to get up, ever, for the rest of my life. Actually, a few text messages did get through, but it almost wasn't worth it, given how my mother had planted herself just outside my door like the prison guard that she was. "Was that a text message sound I just heard? Who texted you, Josh?"

"No one."

"I just hope it wasn't Elizabeth. I swear, Josh, if I find out it was Elizabeth—"

"What? You'll do what? Mom, I'm eighteen. An official adult. And you're insane."

Then I began to think that Mom was right: that if I kept seeing her, I'd end up hurting Elizabeth. I'd crush her with my immense body or hug her to death.

So I stayed home, mainly in bed, with Leo propped up beside me. I was depressed out of my mind, and even after I began to feel better, I couldn't run. All kinds of people came by and visited me and brought me books and CDs that they thought I'd like. Coach Dupe came by maybe half a dozen times, and our rabbi from the synagogue who I hadn't really talked to since my bar mitzvah, and most of my teachers, and Fleur, and my old roommate from the nuthouse, Litton, who I hadn't even really thought much about, and it was amazing, too, because in the nuthouse the dude had barely spoken, but now, as he sat by my bed, he filled me in on everything he was doing, including football, because it turned out that he was a big high school football star, and he had all these teams recruiting him, was set to get a full ride at Rutgers, and the guy looked so good—*built*, with muscles you could see under his clothes and bright white sparkly teeth and beautiful smooth skin the color of oak—he was like a movie star. And then one day after school the chief insect himself came by. Really. Wonders will never cease. He gave me a CD that he'd downloaded all by himself—a mixed tape of his favorite bands, including Radiohead, Mumford and Sons, Rage Against the Machine, and Foo Fighters. Handing it to me, here's what he said: "Sorry, man."

I had terrible nightmares, probably from all the pain meds I was on. Every time I dropped off, I started falling off cliffs and bouncing off additional cliffs, with endless holes of terror opening up to swallow me, one after the next, and then it was my mind itself that was filled with holes, each one more terrible than the next as I fell into the depths of my own understanding of things to discover that life was all a lie—that my entire sense of how things were was a lie, a fantasy, a phantasmagoria, a film. Again and again, I woke up screaming. Then I'd find Leo, lost under the covers, and hug him to my chest.

When at last I was well enough to leave the house, Dr. Rose wanted to know what had made me so afraid. "What exactly did you see in your dreams?" he said. I said that I couldn't remember, and that's because I couldn't.

"You will in time," he said.

22

Elizabeth hadn't been kidding when she said she had something to tell me. When, six weeks later, I finally went back to school, the first thing Elizabeth said was "News."

And I said, "Don't want to know."

And she said, "Don't be stupid."

And I said, "I'm always stupid, okay? That's the point. I'm so stupid that I go around hurting everyone. I'm pretty sure that Sophie must be dead. And they're not telling me. And they don't want me to kill you, too." I hung my head. Elizabeth swatted me.

"Except, man-o-drama, I found Sophie," she said. "And have thus exposed yet another flaw in your thinking."

"You found Sophie? You mean she's not dead?"

"It must be nice to have your own personal guru of brilliance."

You know how in movies they speed up time so you see the hero or heroine going from deepest darkest dismal misery to light and joy and bubbly Champagne happiness when he/she re-falls-in-love with his/her love interest, and even though the time frame is meant to be weeks or months, it takes about thirteen seconds on the screen and is done with light and music? That's how it was, right then, in the math hall at Western High. Except in my case, it really did take only a few seconds. For the first time in months, the light came back on.

"What? What do you mean you found her?"

"I found her, is what I mean. I did a little digging."

"*I* did a little digging. I did *a lot* of digging. How could you find her when I couldn't?"

"It's called not being you, boo-boo," she said. "Here, look."

And then she took out her cell phone and showed me a picture of someone who looked just like Sophie only not. Under her picture were the words "Patient number 223, age nineteen."

"Where'd you get this?"

"Plastic surgeon's website. West Side Plastic Surgery in New York City, to be exact."

"Explain. Please. Please explain."

She pointed at her forehead. "So you see this? Like how I explained to you how I walked through a floor-to-ceiling window when I was running away from the mall cop? And then, how you told me that your brother told you that Sophie was the one who hurt you?"

I was following her and not following her at the same time, and when the bell rang, and the halls began to empty out, we ignored it.

"Because that got me thinking about the subject, about what happens when people are scared. Because like, if one person is threatening, maybe the other person isn't real happy about it?"

"I don't get it."

"Look, Josh. Look closely." That's when I saw it. In the picture. The Sophie who looked like Sophie and simultaneously didn't look like Sophie had a faint line, barely traceable, on her cheek.

"This is the *after* picture," Elizabeth said. "The *before* picture is much much worse."

"And you just happened to come across this website?" I said, squinting so I could read the URL for West Side Plastic Surgery.

"Well, yeah, kind of—I mean, actually, not so much, it was more a matter of persistence. And of being a genius."

"Not following."

She shrugged.

"Seriously. Are you going to enlighten me or just stand there bragging?"

"It's not a brag if it's the truth. Therefore, one, I am a genius, and two, at first I merely had my genius-flash-of-genius insight, vis-à-vis maybe it wasn't *just* you who got banged up during the Sophie episode." She pointed again at her own scar. "Like with me and that asshole— we both got hurt. Me, I got pregnant. But he had to register as a sex offender and spend quality time in prison. And then when Mama told me that between her health insurance having finally kicked in and the money in damages from the county, I can get rid of this scar, we went to this doctor, Dr. Goldberg, this plastic surgeon here in New Jersey, who I really really liked. And anyway she had me look at all these before-and-after pictures, in her office, you see? Which is when the light bulb of genius flashed on a second time. Then Dr. Goldberg told me not to rush into things and urged me to look at the photos on her website."

"So?"

"So if Dr. Goldberg has a website with the before-and-afters maybe other plastic surgeons do too."

"So?"

"So that's how I found Sophie!"

I just stood there and gaped like a fish.

"Just like that?" I said. "Presto, you pushed a couple of buttons on the interweb, and there she is, Sophie, on a plastic surgery website?"

"Not presto, dude. More like hours and hours and hours of looking at pictures until my eyeballs were falling out of my head—tasteless, sorry. But then, all of a sudden, yup: I saw it. This picture. And I just knew it was her. Sophie."

"But why do you think that that's *Sophie*?" I finally said.

"Because it looks like her, that's why."

"How do you know?" And then I remembered, *duh*, that months earlier I'd given her that picture, that one picture of Sophie and me taken at summer camp, for safekeeping.

"It *is* her, isn't it?" she said as I wondered whether I was going to puke or only have a puke-like throat-gagging-moment, because the second Elizabeth asked me, I knew it was: it was Sophie. Right there, on Elizabeth's cell phone's screen. Sophie, who wasn't beautiful, or even close to beautiful, or anything other than nice-looking, but in a distant, bland way, the way people you don't really know look in family photo albums.

"Aren't you going to thank me?"

"Oh my God."

"Fine, I'll take that for now, seeing as that you're obviously completely overwhelmed by my sheer and astonishing brilliance."

"Can I see the *before* picture?"

"Are you sure you want to?" She put her hand on my wrist. I could feel all five of her fingers, separately, curling around it.

I wasn't, but I told her that I was.

The plan was that Elizabeth would make an appointment at West Side Plastic Surgery and I would go with her and when we were there we'd ask the doctor a million questions, especially about patient number 223, age nineteen. Which meant skipping school, which meant that, when my parents found out, I'd be in big doo-doo, but since my life couldn't get all that much more sucky, I risked it.

It was winter. New York City was a brown-and-gray blur. At West Side Plastic Surgery there were bottles of Perrier water and free vials of various creams and lotions. Glass coffee tables were piled high with magazines of perfect-looking women wearing the kinds of clothes that I'd never actually seen on a live female, though maybe I had and hadn't noticed. Elizabeth looked worried. She kept squeezing my hand and then making little coughing noises and swinging her left foot back and forth.

"It's just a doctor," I said. "It's legit."

"I know," she said. "That's what makes me nervous."

When it was Elizabeth's turn, the doctor, a middle-aged man with a lot of curly silver hair, asked Elizabeth to lean back so he could take a good look at her scar, examined it under some kind of special magnifying machine, and touched it very gently with his gloved hands. She began to cry, just a little, but since Elizabeth almost never cried, even her little was a lot. "Does it hurt?" the doctor asked.

"No."

"You're crying," he said.

"I know."

"Do you want to tell me why?"

"No."

"Is he a relative?" he said, indicating me with a nod of my head.

"Best friend."

"Okay," the doctor said. "Just one more minute and we'll talk."

Afterward Elizabeth explained what I had already kind of figured out, which was that every time someone touched her scar, it just brought all the awfulness back—but for now I just want to say that Dr. Alfonzo (that was the doctor's name) had three separate notebooks for Elizabeth to look at, because, as it turned out, he specialized in what he called "youth repair." Most of his patients, he said, had been involved in accidents of some sort, mainly car accidents, but other things, too: roller-blading accidents, kitchen accidents, sports accidents, dog bites, skiing collisions. "I'm going to send you and your friend across the hall with my nurse, who'll show you the notebooks," he said. "There's no rush. Take your time. Think about what you want to do, and who you want to work with. Okay?"

"Okay," Elizabeth said.

"This way," the nurse said.

He wasn't kidding when he said he'd done a lot of "youth repair." In the notebooks were page after page of before and after pictures, some of them like miracles, with the before looking like a Halloween mask and the after looking like a normal kid. And then, at last, in the second notebook, we came upon patient number 223, age nineteen.

"What happened to her?" Elizabeth said.

"Let's see, oh yes," the nurse said, biting her top lip. "That was unusual."

"What do you mean?" Elizabeth said, smooth as silk even though I was afraid I'd piss myself.

"Very strange situation," she said. "She'd been attacked, this one. By someone who'd had—I think she said he'd been stalking her for months. Some guy who was obsessed with her and insisted that they had to get married. She'd been terrified of him—and then, this happened. What is this world coming to, huh?"

"No kidding," said Elizabeth.

"Sorry," the nurse then said. "I shouldn't have told you any of that."

"It's okay," Elizabeth said. "Weird stuff happens."

"But Dr. Alfonzo did a good job, don't you think?" the nurse said, gesturing toward the after photo.

"She looks good," Elizabeth said.

"You will too," the nurse said.

"Not *that* good."

"You'd be surprised."

"In my dreams," Elizabeth said.

"And your mom? Your dad? They couldn't come with you today?" the nurse said.

"Mom works, and my dad passed," Elizabeth white-lied. "Which is why I brought my bud here, instead."

"No problem," the nurse said, and then, bending down in a fake whisper so I could hear too, she added, "He's cute, your friend. Are you guys dating?"

Elizabeth said, "In *his* dreams."

23

*O*n the train going home, Elizabeth said that she liked Dr. Alfonso so much that she was leaning toward having him do her plastic surgery, unless I didn't want her to go to the same doctor that Sophie had gone to.

"No," I said on autopilot, "it's totally your decision." And yes, I *would* have said the same thing had I been thinking clearly, but it took days for me to think clearly again—days before I could fully digest the unalterable and incontrovertible fact that someone had attacked Sophie, and that that someone, clearly, had been me. But instead I let my eye and brain slide out of focus while brown and dreary New Jersey slipped by the streaked and smudged windows in all its brown and dreary dreariness: the huddle of brown-gray houses culminating in the brown-gray, car-streaked cluster of Newark; the backs of triple-deckers; the wide expanse of industrial wastelands; poisoned rivers shimmering with oily rainbow slicks; cattails; feral cats; heavy equipment; abandoned bicycles; rusted-out cars.

The Garden State.

The weeks crawled by: algebra; chemistry; English; lunch; Mom yelling at Nate; Nate yelling at Dad; Coach Dupe patting me on the shoulder; Shaw Street CVS Stop N Shop Starbucks Essen Park Goose Park the Skinny Deli the synagogue the Catholic church the Methodist church the Episcopal church the playground the tennis courts the pond the train station the commuters the elementary school and little kids and dogs and cats and ladies out gardening as my running shoes *pound, pound, pound* and I run three miles four miles five miles six, seven—and Elizabeth; Elizabeth; Elizabeth—because we still met every lunch—and talk talk talk talk and Elizabeth saying that I'll remember but I don't and at TITSS meetings I'm bored and at school kids are coming up to me asking me how I am, are you doing better, Josh, are you are you are you looking good Josh no I mean it listen we're getting together for pizza after school if you want to join us and I'm really sorry if and you know and okay see you later no worries . . .

January, February, March, April.

And then it happened.

Dinner was spinach and eggplant all swirled around in a gooey brown sauce because Dad had decided he needs to eat even more vegetables because he didn't want to get cancer like his father and his uncle did and die before sixty, but Mom was like *Do you know how hard it is to please all three of you?* So we also had French bread and a green salad and beans for protein but I just wasn't hungry. I hadn't really been hungry since that trip to New York with Elizabeth, plus eating nothing but vegetables gave me stomach aches, and anyway, the only time I felt anything more than dumb-and-numb is when I was running: running just to run; running to feel the pain in my legs and the pain in my lungs and the sweat pouring off my hairline and down my sides and coming home exhausted with my breath and heart pounding in my ears. The running blotted out WHAT HAPPENED? WHAT HAPPENED? WHAT HAPPENED? All I heard was _____. Or maybe: Better study for to-morrow's quiz. Or: stir-fried tofu again?

Which was so much better than before, so much better that even the small "v" voices had ceased screaming, contenting themselves to mere murmurs, ceaseless, relentless, but not so loud.

Now Mom was going: "Really, Josh, I worry about how you eat. You need to eat more. You've lost enough weight—and really, hon, my hat's off to you—and I think I speak for both me and Daddy when I say we're just so proud of you, of all you've accomplished this year, and especially how you're mastering your own fate again, taking hold of the reigns, you know." Her voice drifted off for approximately a one-kerbillionth of a nanosecond before she said, "What's with the face, Nate?"

"I need meat, Mom. I'm a growing boy, remember?"

"I know, but your dad's off meat."

"And maybe if you fed us meat now and then maybe just maybe Josh would eat. Because, Mom, have you thought of that?"

"I have thought of that, Nate. But your father is on this health kick."

"I'm not on a health kick," Dad said. "But as I've explained before, and any reasonable person would know, a diet based on plant foods is healthier for you than one based on animal products, especially meat. We eat too much cheese around here too."

Out of nowhere, Mom exploded: "For God's sake! I just can't do this anymore! What with trying to cater to your dietary anxieties, keep the house running, deal with Josh's ongoing challenges, and worrying about Elizabeth, it's insane!"

"Calm down," Dad said.

"Calm? I'm not the one who freaks out if pot roast is served!" Mom said. "Freaking out over pot roast when our entire family is teetering on the precipice! It's like worrying about practicing the piano when an army is about to invade."

"Enough!"

"And that girl, she's only, what? Five foot one? Two? Josh is twice her size. And with a baby! She's no bigger than a baby herself!"

And with that, the entire table fell silent. Dead silent. Silence like during a funeral. Silence like after the bomb.

"Mother?" I finally said. "What difference could it make that Elizabeth is small?"

Mom tried to make light of it. "Nothing," she said. "Just that I worry about what could happen, if, you know . . ."

The seconds ticked by, the minutes, the hours until Nate spoke.

"It's 'cause of how you stalked Sophie."

"Silence!" It was Dad.

"They're afraid you're going to do the same thing to Elizabeth," Nate said.

"Shut up this instant!"

Nate turned a bright purple pink and began to cry. "No!" he said. "I won't shut up! It's not fair and you know it! I have to live here too, you know! But no, it's all these secrets, all these things that really happened and are really happening only no one can say anything around here because we're all supposed to go tip-toeing around the truth, because what if one of us slips up and Josh goes all bonkers again? Because you know what? It isn't my fault, it isn't my responsibility if Josh goes nuts again, okay? What happened to him isn't my fault!"

"No one said it was."

"You didn't have to say it, though, did you? No, not with all your telling me to shut up, and every time I told you that Josh was acting weird, you said I was wrong, I was jealous, or selfish, or competing with him. And even now, if Josh does one thing that upsets you, it's somehow *my* fault."

"What are you even talking about, Nate?"

"Like that one time he went to the city, and you blamed me."

"But you knew about it, and we didn't. You should have tried to stop him."

"Or how about his being friends with Elizabeth to begin with who by the way is just this girl, and okay, maybe she's weird, what do I know? But she's just this *girl*, okay, but somehow it's my job to babysit Josh so he won't go near her? I mean it, that's FUCKED."

"We're in this together, Nate," Dad said. "You know that."

"We're a *family*," Mom echoed. "We need to be here for each other. To operate as a team."

"We're a messed-up family, is what we are," Nate said. "I just hate you guys sometimes. I really really really hate you sometimes."

For a moment I wondered if Nate was including me in the "you guys" or just our parents, but I couldn't really follow that thought through because instead of thinking I was reacting, up on my feet and so angry I could barely speak so instead of speaking I kind of stammered/spit/sobbed that I already knew that I'd hurt Sophie that I knew she'd had to go to the plastic surgeon and that she'd been the one who'd taken out my eye except that I just couldn't remember, not really, not *remember* remember, like the memory belonged to me versus what it now was, which was a series of fact points that I had strung together to make a narrative, but then the room went *whoosh whoosh whoosh* around me and it all came back.

24

There was one fact, and only one fact. In the entire universe, there was only one fact. And that fact was that Sophie and I were to be joined, forever, in bliss, and our bliss would expand and explode into the universe, sending shivers of unending and profound joy to each atom, to each quivering molecule, into the hearts of all creatures, dead and alive, and into the very bosom of God Himself.

Sophie was destiny. I was Sophie's all.

The word "love" did not convey the power, the force, that drove us together, that brought us together, that commanded that we fuse, that we merge, that we blend, that we bring forth the better world, the new tomorrow, the beauty that lay hidden behind every commonplace assumption and thing.

It was decreed.

And though I was merely a human vessel, frail in my human body, frail in my youth, frail in my limitations, I'd been given the task, the great task to give birth to this new beauty . . . with Sophie.

Sophie, the beloved.

Sophie, who completed me.

Our love was bigger than both of us, bigger than the entire world.

It was easy to escape the confines of home. Mom was working late. Dad was working late. Nate was busy homework friends running Frisbee pizza TV where you going Josh Mom and Dad said you need to stay home tonight remember no really I mean it Josh you can't just split like that they'll kill me where are you going come back come back!

It isn't Nate's fault though that he does not have access to the greatness beyond, that he hasn't been chosen, as I have, for the great mission, and so I merely shrug, just me, Josh, inside my Josh-body that is also merely the human costume I wear during my incarnated time on earth and inside my Josh body where I am like all other human creatures I reach for my wallet and buy a train ticket and ride the train to Penn Station and then take the subway to West Fourth Street and walk the four blocks to Sophie's dorm where she and her roommate are on the fifth floor and then all I have to do is wait for the security guard to turn his back and up I go up the flights of stairs I will not take the elevator there are security cameras in the elevator the elevator stops and starts and the elevator is dangerous but the stairs are quiet hushed dusty cool I take them two at a time and when I get to Sophie's room, the door is open. Just a crack.

Hi Sophie I love you Sophie. But she's not in her room. The lights are on, her books are spread out, her computer's on, I just have to wait for her to come back.

Here she comes, I can hear her now, she's talking with someone in the hall, something about a concert, Bach, Beethoven, piano, she loves music, but she's got to finish her stupid philosophy paper why did she sign up to take a philosophy course she hates philosophy whose stupid idea was it for her to take a philosophy course anyway oh well she better get to it. That's what she's saying. All her words. All her college student words. The One tells me what to do: to wait for her behind the door. To close the door behind her when she comes in.

When she comes in, more words, false words, she does not understand what she is saying: Oh my God! Get out of here! NOW!

I love you.

Leave now or I call the police.

No you won't you love me, love me, we are love, we are the hope . . .

She doesn't know that it's too late to stop the progress, the progression of unity, because she's reaching past me, toward her desk, for her cell phone on her desk but I've got her now and she's leaning into me all lovelovelovelove so much love there is she knows it now I know she knows it because we are together, our skins, skin to skin and I'm on top she's on bottom I'm on bottom she's on top we're turning and tumbling the door I love you the floor I love love love she's right here mine.

And then agony. Agony. Blood agony. Blood in my brain. Blood in my mouth. Blood on my tongue and blood everywhere a blood sacrifice.

In her hands she has a pen, a pen dripping with blood, my blood. A ballpoint pen. A pen. Blood.

She's screaming: Stop stop stop STOP STOP STOP STOP!

Now I understand: it's a blood sacrifice, a dual blood sacrifice, together we will anoint with our comingled blood, and I am Angel/Beast Angel/Satan and I have no weapon but my love for her, her face in my mouth, her face between my teeth.

OH MY GOD YOU BIT ME and she too is bleeding, bleeding from her face, her jaw, our blood mingling together, hers and mine, a dual sacrifice to save the world.

And the next thing I remembered, I woke up in the hospital, a hole where my left eye used to be.

25

What I told Dr. Rose, and what I'd already told Elizabeth and Coach Dupe and Elizabeth's mother and even Nate and a bunch of random kids at TITSS, was that the worst thing I could ever know about myself was also the best thing, or rather, *knowing* the worst thing was the best thing. It's like I was trapped in a cave, and I thought the cave was the whole world, but then I came out of the cave, and saw the world.

Elizabeth said, "Well, at least you aren't a rapist."

"Only because she stabbed me first."

"Wish I'd thought of that with Barry," she said. "Stabbing him right in the eyeball, I mean."

To which I said nothing, because I still felt so horrible, so ashamed, so appalled. But at the same time, light.

"Plus you so didn't kill anyone."

"You didn't either."

"True that."

By now Elizabeth was taking Angela with her everywhere, no longer pretending that she was just an ordinary high school girl with nothing more on her mind than her SAT scores. One day, when Elizabeth and I went out for a slice, a former insect saw the two of us and Angela, and came over. "Wow, he's so cute!"

"She," Elizabeth said. "She's a she."

"She—she's so cute."

Elizabeth grinned.

It was amazing, how normal we were, me and Elizabeth and Angela, and the whole little world of Blooming Acres swirling around, doing what it does, and me with my big huge awful past and Elizabeth with hers, and both of us just sitting there, eating pizza.

I'd do anything to have never met Sophie. To have left her alone. I don't even know why I loved her so much. I mean, at first—when we first met, at camp—I did have this humongous crush on her. Because she was just—she was cute: with all that dark wild curly hair, those dark wild flashing eyes, and smart too, off to NYU, and Beethoven-this and Bach-that. Like a girl in a poem. Not that I read poetry. Poetry was totally lame.

Even though I lost my eye, I'm glad she stopped me, I'm glad she speared my eyeball with her Paper Mate ballpoint pen and I lost so much blood I passed out so I couldn't hurt her anymore. When she screamed, when she opened the door, when the EMS came—there must have been crowds of people in there, the ambulance crew, a team for her, a team for me, only I guess I was the only one who could've bled to death. Whereas Sophie—a normal girl who just wanted to go to college and who'd never loved me or even really liked me and in fact grew to hate me and who had had a restraining order put out against me and who did everything she could to keep me away from her—Sophie had a huge gash, a gash I'd put there with my teeth, in her left cheek.

Her cheek. My eye.

"I see," Dr. Rose said. "Good work, Josh. Good work."

"Do you think I could write to her? Tell her how sorry I am?"

"Probably not. Not with a restraining order."

"But how can I make it up to her? What I did to her?"

"It's just something you're going to have to live with."

"Always?"

"Always is an awfully long time," Dr. Rose said. "But you'll figure it out."

Even without infinity stretching out before me, things at home pretty well sucked. Mom and Dad fought all the time—and when I say all the time, I mean whenever they were in the same room, which thankfully wasn't all that often, as Dad left early in the morning for work and half the time didn't come home until after dinner. And that was because Mom had gone back to cooking normal food, like chicken and pot roast, and Dad said that she was trying to kill him, that with his high blood pressure and getting older he was merely trying to stay healthy, to which she said that he was merely trying to control her, to which Nate said that the problem was that both Mom and Dad were trying to control everything all the time, and that he, for one, thank God, was going to be out of there soon.

It was true, too. Nate had gotten into a whole bunch of colleges, plus he had been recruited to run for GW and also for Connecticut College, which was good, because Mom and Dad were almost out of money. So he was kind of pissed at me, too, because if it hadn't been for me, Mom and Dad wouldn't have been almost out of money.

"Legal fees, mainly," Mom finally explained one day after yet another round of bickering, complaining, and pissed-off-ness. "Sophie's parents took us to court, for negligence. Sophie had a restraining order, but as you now know it didn't exactly restrain you."

"Do you really need to go into all the details?" Dad said from the other room. "Do you really think it's a good idea to make him feel even guiltier than he already feels?"

Which is when Mom burst into tears of her own, saying, "Enough! I can't stand it! Nate was right—Josh was right—all these secrets. We just can't do this anymore! That's the problem in this house, these secrets, and not whether you eat meat or Josh secretly sleeps with a stuffed bunny."

"His name is Leo," I said.

"And anyway," Mom said, mopping up her tears with a stained dish towel, "once you did what you did, Sophie's parents went nuts, can't blame them really, and they were going to sue us for you name it—go after the house, all our assets, the whole bit—you were still seventeen, see, a minor in our household. So in the long run they agreed that if you disappeared from Sophie's life forever, they'd drop the charges. You terrified her, son. I still have the letter she wrote!"

"Letter?" I said. "A letter from Sophie! Let me see it!"

"I don't know, honey. I shouldn't have even mentioned it."

"Let me see it!"

"No," Dad said. "That's not for your eyes."

"Eye," Nate said.

"I think I deserve to know about my own damn history," I said.

A minute later, the thing was in my hand, typed, double-spaced, and to the point:

Dear Mr. and Mrs. Cushing,

Please make Josh stop following me around. I've tried

to tell him in every way that he's scaring me, but he just

won't listen. I turn around, and there he is: in my dorm,

in the cafeteria, outside my English lit class. I just

started college and I can barely concentrate on my classes

because no matter where I go or what I do, there he is,

just waiting for me. You have to understand: I don't hate

him, but I'm afraid. I'm five foot three. Josh is over six

feet and an athlete! Please. Please stop him! I don't know

what to do!

Sincerely,

Sophie Luxer

"We were all just terrified," Mom said. "And as you know, it got worse—way worse. You hurt her, Josh. You really hurt her."

"And you thought I'd do the same thing to Elizabeth?"

"After what she'd already been through. I didn't know what to do, Josh. I had to protect her. I had to try."

What could I say? By the time we got to this conversation, Mom was sobbing so much that she was soaking the chair she sat on, soaking the floor, her tears running down her face and into the walls and the woodwork and the pipes, dripping into the basement.

I exaggerate. But you get the drift.

"And she was, well, you have to admit—well, it's true, that at first what concerned me was *her* record, her own history—which isn't 100 percent savory, you know?"

"I know, Mom. But Elizabeth didn't do anything wrong."

"But how was I to know that? I mean, eventually, yes, I got access to the record, and I saw the court records. But after what I've seen, myself, in my own practice, these poor kids, these teenagers, no older than you and Nate, and what they've been through, and what animals some of them become, you can't blame the kids, but still." And she'd go on like that, telling me about this and that pro bono client she'd taken on through child welfare, and all their stories got mingled together in my mind, until it was just one big story of adults slamming their kids around and kids going wild in response, one big story of despair, hopelessness, misery.

I quit going to the TITSS meetings. They were just too depressing.

I started hanging out with Litton, my nuthouse roommate. He got a scholarship to play football for the University of Wisconsin.

Elizabeth decided to go to Rutgers, Newark, and study nursing. Her plastic surgery—she ended up staying with Dr. Goldberg, in New Jersey—was outstanding.

Nate decided to run for GW, in Washington, DC.

And I failed, a second time, to graduate from high school. I was short one credit.

26

And so, dear Admissions Committee, you now know why it took me such a long time to get around to applying to college, having missed the first deadline on account of being out of my gourd, and the second on account of failing to get my high school degree and also not really caring all that much about it to begin with.

I spent my "gap year" as a full-time nanny, watching Angela from around eight in the morning, when her mother went to school and her grandmother went to her new, much better job—as a guidance counselor—until around four. Also, I finished that one last credit, in US government, and took a couple of classes at community college. In my free time, I ran. I also went to see Dr. Rose, fought with my parents, walked Buster, and volunteered, as the assistant-to-the-assistant coach at Western High. Coach Dupe, as you'll see, is one of my references. He insists that I run cross-country again in college, but I frankly don't think it would be fair to the other runners: after all, I've got two years of seniority on them. And also, I'm done with competition. Let Nate compete—which he does—and win the trophies—which he also does. Let Litton triumph on the turf, and let Mom get out there and struggle and argue and compete and win, too, which she does, often and regularly, at the Essex County courthouse. Let Dad get out there and blow them away—at the synagogue, anyway—with his awesome original Rosh Hashanah and Shabbat songs, with his amazing guitar licks. Me, I just want to learn about how the world operates, and why humans are the way we are. That's why I'm applying to college.